His Father's Last Gift

A Darcy and Elizabeth Variation

LEENIE BROWN

Leenie B Books

Halifax

Copyright

Contents

Chapter 1

IT WAS A BEAUTIFUL November morning. The sun was bright, heavy dew – not frost – covered the ground, and the air was so crisp that it nearly crackled. It was in this wonderfully tranquil setting of perfection that Fitzwilliam Darcy drew in a deep, cleansing breath of solitude and released it in a puff of vapour reminiscent of the fog that rose lazily above the moors on a morning such as this. Nothing. Absolutely nothing was so refreshing as a solitary ride in the early hours of the day.

As he relaxed into the rhythmic undulation of his horse's movements, he had to admit to himself that his decision to not ask his friend, Charles Bingley, to accompany him this morning had been a most excellent notion, for it meant that, for the past hour, Darcy had not heard even one word spoken about the lovely Miss Bennets who were currently ensconced in one of Netherfield's many guest rooms.

And just like that, as he approached the stables, Darcy's mind sprang from its repose to once again twist, turn, and completely jumble itself around the thought of the youngest Miss Bennet in residence at Netherfield – Miss Elizabeth.

How had he ever declared her to be merely tolerable? He shook his head at his ignorance as he dismounted from his horse.

He had tried to excuse himself for such an utter lack of perception for days now, but he could not. At least, not completely. The only thing which he could credit for his stupidity was the fact that her beauty was not the sort that could be captured by a painter's talent, and, therefore, he had missed it upon his first cursory glance in her direction at the assembly in Meryton. There had been a throng of people – dancing, talking, pushing past one another as they moved through the hall. The whole ordeal had been rather overwhelming to Darcy's sensibilities. It was not that he was unused to a crush of people at a soiree for London boasted many such affairs. However, no ballroom had ever felt as stifling as that one in Meryton had that night.

It was due, of course, to his state of mind and not the reality of the situation, but still, he was going to count it as a worthy excuse for his oversight regarding Miss Elizabeth's charm.

Now that he had had ample opportunities to consider her more closely, he naturally saw his error. He did not understand it, but he did see it. To scrutinize Miss Elizabeth from an artistic point of view, as he had attempted to several times now, her features were nothing out of the ordinary – they were neither deficient nor striking. However, if one watched her long enough – and Darcy had watched her a great deal – the animation of her eyes and their expression when reflecting her pleasure or displeasure was a momentary and delightful glimpse of her exquisite beauty which shone from within, and that fascinating, desirable, enchanting allure was not something which could be readily captured in flat paintings or cold stone sculptures. That would take a master of the highest order to even attempt it, and yet, even then, such a great artist would still struggle to capture the essence of her loveliness.

Darcy handed his horse over to a groom and turned toward the garden. He would forestall his return to the house for a few more minutes. Neither of Bingley's sisters would be below stairs yet, but they would be soon, and he would rather not be the first one to greet them. Caroline, Bingley's youngest and only unwed sister, seemed more determined than ever to tease him into liking her.

Darcy could not fathom why she thought she could do that. It was not as if he had ever responded in a fashion designed to give her hope. Indeed, he attempted to do just the opposite, so why did she continue to annoy him with her teasing?

Ladies made very little sense to him. It was a failing that he had thought was of little significance until his sister started to blossom into a young lady. Her sweetness had faded for a time. Her demands had become sharper and harder to deny without creating a tense and unpleasant atmosphere between them.

He blew out a puff of frustration – it was not as noticeable a puff as his exhalation had been earlier. The air here as he approached the wildwood portion of Netherfield's gardens must be warmer than that which he had encountered in the fields. Or, it was quite possible that the sun's warmth was beginning to reach further toward the ground.

As he contemplated his sister and the challenge it was to completely understand her at times, he rounded a bend in the informal path that wove its way through the wildwood and paused for a moment to take in the view before continuing his ramble.

This was his favourite portion of the whole estate. It was sheltered and quiet. The shadows of the nearly bare branches of the trees danced overhead in the breeze, and he watched them as he rounded a second bend in the path. And came face to face with the very person who had sent him on his solitary ride to sort out his thoughts.

"Oh! Mr. Darcy!" The very person who had sent him riding alone to sort out his thoughts, stepped neatly to the side of the path, thereby avoiding colliding with him. "It is a surprise to see you here."

"Miss Elizabeth." Darcy offered a shallow bow of greeting to the startled lady before him. "How is your sister today?"

"I fear she is little better than she was last evening. However, she is, at least, no worse. Her fever has not grown hotter, and her voice is no weaker than it was."

"I am happy to hear her illness has not become more serious, but I am sorry she is still unwell."

"As am I." Miss Elizabeth offered him a small smile. "I have just sent a note to my mother asking her to come see Jane and decide what should be done. Jane would dearly love to be at home instead of being a bother to Miss Bingley and her brother."

A bother? That was a word which was far removed from anything Darcy had ever thought of Miss Bennet. As far as he could tell, she had been little trouble at all. Miss Elizabeth had seen to her care, and, to his knowledge, there had been no special requests made. "Does your sister feel herself to be an imposition?"

Miss Elizabeth's captivating fine eyes sparkled with amusement. "She does, but you must not tell anyone that she has complained. She would be mortified to be spoken of in such a fashion."

"And yet, *you*, who knows that she would be so affected, have just cast her in such an unwelcome light." Darcy allowed his lips to curl into a small grin as he teased the lady who had occupied a great deal of his waking thoughts for the past three weeks.

Her eyes narrowed as she studied him. Her expression did not, however, completely lose its amused appearance. "I would think you were finding fault with me were it not for your smile."

"I am not disparaging," he assured her quickly. "Though to be completely honest, it does seem odd that you would share with me something about your sister of which you think she would not approve." He held her gaze and saw her lips twitch.

"I would likely suffer a great shock, Mr. Darcy – one from which recovery might not be possible – were you not to think it strange," she replied. "Others might not even notice, but you are a gentleman of great perception, are you not?"

His small grin grew into a full smile. "I would like to think so, but I have proof that I am not nearly as perceptive as I should be." His smile faltered as he contemplated first his inability to see Elizabeth's beauty and then, his younger sister's near ruin. He was far from perceptive – no matter how much he wished he could claim Miss Elizabeth's words to be true.

He shook his head to clear it of such things. Miss Elizabeth was teasing him, and he did not want to miss a moment of that. He would contemplate his failures later. Her teasing was so much more enjoyable than that of Miss Bingley. He motioned to the path they were on. "Walk with me?"

She nodded and fell in step with him.

"Will you tell me why you have chosen to share that your sister is not completely at ease with her current circumstances?" He clasped his hands behind his back to keep from offering her his arm. They were acquaintances and making such an offer would not be shocking. Indeed, it would be readily welcomed by most females he had met. However, Miss Elizabeth had, most surprisingly, refused his offer to dance at Lucas Lodge, and he had not come upon a female who refused him as a dance partner before that evening. Based on that fact, he guessed that Miss Elizabeth would likely be happier to walk unassisted, for she was not like any lady he knew.

"Because it is the truth, and it is justifiable that she should be less than agreeable in all things when she is suffering as she is. It is quite the natural thing for a person to wish to be at home where all is comforting and familiar when one is ill."

"But do you not fear that in speaking so openly about your sister's feelings you will cause me to think poorly of you?"

She turned her face towards him so that when he looked to the side, he saw her full, startled expression rather than just the brim of her bonnet and her profile.

"No," she said with a shake of her head.

"Why?"

She laughed lightly. It was not an altogether friendly sound. In fact, it had a bitter edge to it.

"Because I already know that I am beneath your notice, as is the rest of the neighbourhood. Therefore, I have no fear of lowering myself in your esteem for I have never had it."

Darcy drew back at her words. They were not spoken in a vicious or biting fashion but were, rather, said with the matter-of-factness of a tutor relating a truth to his pupil.

"I do not think meanly of you," he protested. He thought rather well of her – far more well of her than he likely should. Indeed, he was beginning to feel as if he was in some danger of falling in love with her, which, of course, was preposterous. A gentleman should know a lady for longer than a few weeks in which they had only met a handful of times before losing his heart. Or more precisely, a gentleman such as himself, who was not Bingley, should.

"I did not say you thought meanly of me, sir. I merely said that I have never been held in any sort of high esteem. It is not as if you find me *intolerable*."

Darcy closed his eyes and flinched as if he had been slapped. She had heard his words at the assembly, and they had done what he had wanted at the time. She had not expected him to address her in any sort of romantic fashion then, nor did she now. For some reason, that last part bothered him more than it should.

"You are far more than tolerable," he said.

She gave him a look that said she did not believe him.

"I speak the truth."

That did not change how she was looking at him.

"I sorely regret my unkind and ignoble words from our first meeting."

"Do you?"

He saw her smile and shake her head as if laughing at his confession.

"I do. Why do you not believe me?"

"Why should I? I know very little about you, and what I do know, I find rather confusing."

Why should she believe him? He stopped walking and contemplated that. To what could he point as a reason to trust that what he said was true? Try as he might, he could not come up with any compelling reason. That needed to be changed.

She had stopped several steps away from him and had turned to look at him. He met her expectant, and was that a slightly defiant, look? Did she expect him to immediately rebuff her? She would be disappointed.

"You are correct," he admitted. "I cannot come up with one reason why you should believe me to be anything more than my words have indicated I am. I am truly sorry that I have behaved so badly. I hope that with time I can improve in your opinion and earn your forgiveness."

Her lips parted as her jaw dropped somewhat. Perhaps she was not disappointed by his reply so much as surprised.

"Have I shocked you?"

"Somewhat." A crease formed between her eyes as she drew her eyebrows together over a perplexed expression. "And you have confused my thoughts about you even further."

"Did you not expect me to apologize for my reprehensible behaviour?"

Her brow furrowed. "Honestly, no."

Her words slashed at his heart. How had he allowed himself to be so disagreeable that a lady like Miss Elizabeth would not expect him to feel the weight of his errors enough to apologize for them? They were standing well within the bounds of the formal garden, and before she could elaborate on her answer further or he could respond to it, the sound of horses' hooves on the drive reached them, and she turned toward the sound.

"Has Mama arrived already?" she asked. "I did not think I was gone from the house so long."

"I did not hear a carriage," Darcy said. "Would your mother arrive on horseback?"

"No, I dare say she would not."

"Then, it is not your mother."

"I wonder who it could be, then?" She walked toward the border of the garden that would give a good view of the front of the house.

Darcy hurried after her.

"Who is that?" she asked. "He does not look familiar to me at all."

While the person swinging down from his horse did not look familiar to Miss Elizabeth, Darcy knew him well. "That is my cousin."

"Your cousin?" Miss Elizabeth's attention turned from the rider to Darcy.

He nodded. "Colonel Richard Fitzwilliam. Shall we go greet him?"

"I suppose it seems the appropriate thing to do. At least, it is the thing for *you* to do."

Darcy scowled. "Are you dismissing me?"

Miss Elizabeth laughed. "No, I am curious about your cousin and anxious to meet him, but it is best if you greet him now and I meet him later." She sighed and looked longingly at the garden. "I should check on Jane. She was sleeping when I left her, but I have been gone for some time."

"If your sister is sleeping, you could complete your circuit of the garden before you return to the house," Darcy offered softly, earning him a lovely smile.

"You are very perplexing."

"I do not see how."

"Your actions this morning are not what I thought they would be based on our previous meetings."

"I have only been rude once. I have been civil, if not more than civil, at all other times." At least, he had been in her company. Heat crept up his neck at the thought of the unguarded and unkind comments he had made in private.

"Have you not looked to find fault with me and my family?"

Darcy rubbed the back of his neck. "Yes."

"Then, the truth of my statement stands."

Darcy sighed. "I apologize. That was also wrong of me to do." He did not turn his eyes away from her as she held his gaze and looked as if she was weighing what he had said. Hopefully, she would accept his apology and they could move forward with the tentative friendship they seemed to be forming.

Her brow pinched together before she asked softly, "Why did you ask me to dance at Lucas Lodge?"

That was an easy question to answer. However, before he could say more than, "Because..." the sound of a carriage on the driveway interrupted him.

"Mama must be here."

"Most likely."

Miss Elizabeth looked as if she wanted to leave him and fly to the house, but she stood where she was, waiting for his explanation.

"I asked you to dance because I wished to dance with you. I should have danced with you at the assembly. I have long since regretted that decision."

"Darcy!" Richard called from the edge of the garden.

"I must go." Though he did not want to.

"So must I," Miss Elizabeth said, but she hesitated as if she also did not want their interlude to end. "You truly wanted to dance with me? You were not just humouring Sir William?"

Darcy smiled and shook his head. "I truly wanted to dance with you." He still did, and dancing was not on his list of favourite things to do, so it was rather surprising to think he longed to dance at all.

Her lips curved into a pleased smile while her eyes registered her surprise. "Then, perhaps I will not refuse you the next time you ask." She cast a look towards his cousin who was approaching. "I must go to Mama and Jane. Tell Colonel Fitzwilliam that I look forward to meeting him." She dipped a quick curtsey and took her leave.

Chapter 2

DARCY STOOD SILENTLY AS he was, watching Miss Elizabeth leave him, until his cousin was at his side. Only then did he turn from his observation of her to greet Richard. "I did not expect to see you."

"Who was that? Bingley does not have a third sister whom I have not met, does he?"

Darcy chuckled. "No, thank God, he does not."

"Shall we take a turn of the garden?" Richard asked as he swept his hand forward to indicate that they should walk the path on which they stood and then started walking before Darcy could reply. "Has Miss Bingley been a trial?"

"When is she not?"

"I thought you got on well with her at times."

"I abide her without complaint at times. That is not the same as getting on well." It was not that he always found Caroline Bingley abhorrent, but she did have her moments.

"I suppose that is true," Richard admitted. "And all that information does nothing to help me discover the identity of your mystery companion. It is not the usual thing to see you alone in a garden with a lady."

"As you well know, it is not precisely safe to be in the garden with a lady without a chaperone for someone of my fortune."

"It is not safe when you have less fortune but your father has a title, like mine does," Richard agreed with a laugh. "But then not all ladies are scheming, and I take it whomever your companion was is not the sort who wishes to snare you?"

"You are correct about that. Her name is Miss Elizabeth Bennet, and her father's estate, Longbourn, is just three miles from here."

"Then, why is she here instead of at her father's estate? You cannot convince me that Miss Bingley has befriended a possible rival for your affections. Are you certain this Miss Bennet is not scheming to trap you?"

Darcy shook his head and chuckled as he turned toward the house. "No, Miss Bingley has not befriended Miss Elizabeth. However, she has made overtures of befriending Miss Elizabeth's elder sister, who, as it happens, fell ill while visiting with Miss Bingley and Mrs. Hurst on Tuesday and is now convalescing in one of Netherfield's guest rooms. Miss Elizabeth arrived yesterday to care for her sister."

"Aaaah." The word was drawn out as if everything now made sense to him. It was a word and tone that usually declared to Darcy that his cousin was taking the information given to him and extrapolating scenarios from it. There was always danger in that small word when uttered by Richard.

"What do you think you know?" It was usually best to have Richard's ideas in the open rather than allowing him to expand and expound upon them in his mind.

Richard's smile as he answered was smug. "Miss Bingley should be on her guard, for her hope of securing you has diminished."

"She never had a hope of securing me."

"Yes, I know, but if she had, it would have been ground to dust by the arrival of a pretty young lady who cares for her sister." He chuckled. "You do have a soft spot for all those who care for their siblings."

That was true, but he had good reason for it, for, to him, it spoke well of a person's character if they cared for others.

"I am not at all certain she would have made the effort for any of her other sisters as she has for Miss Bennet. They seem to be exceptionally close."

"Any of her *other sisters*? How many are there?"

"There are five Bennet daughters in total."

"Five?"

Darcy nodded. "No brothers."

"None?"

Darcy shook his head. "No. Just five daughters. Miss Bennet is, of course, the eldest. Then, there is Miss Elizabeth. Both Miss Bennet and Miss Elizabeth appear to be proper young ladies."

"But the other three do not?"

If only they did! But sadly, from what Darcy had seen, they did not, or, at least, they did not completely.

"Miss Mary, who is the next eldest after Miss Elizabeth, is quite serious and eager to gain approval through displaying her accomplishments." Truly, Miss Mary only lacked some refinement, a little softening. He did not doubt that she was capable of being a very proper young miss.

"Miss Kitty, who is after Miss Mary, is the shadow of her youngest sister Miss Lydia." He blew out a great breath. Miss Lydia was the true issue. "Miss Lydia is about Georgiana's age, though she could pass for older to look at her." It was a fact that she seemed to know and flaunt, and that many of the unattached gentlemen in the area admired. "However, when she speaks, you would think she was younger than Georgie."

"Am I to decipher from this explanation that Miss Lydia is silly?

Darcy nodded. "Much like her mother."

"Oh, I see. Are you saying Mrs. Bennet and her youngest are like some mothers and debutantes that we know in town?"

"Precisely. Do you remember Miss Fisher or Miss Kelly?"

There had been several suggestions of possible matches each season from Richard's mother, Lady Matlock – she was forever attempting to match either him or Richard with someone. A few of them, including Miss Fisher and her mother and Miss Kelly and her mother, had been declared by Lord Matlock to be far too silly to be married by anyone with an ounce of sense who wished to retain that sense. Darcy and Richard had agreed, of course, because it was true.

"Who could forget them? Does this mean Miss Bingley's position of being hopeful that she can snare you is not in danger?"

They had reached the house by this time, and as they stood in front of it, Darcy scrubbed his face with his hands. "For the moment." Was that even true? He shook his head. "I think I need to return to town."

If he stayed here, there was likely no hope for him to escape without either a broken heart or being tied to a mother and sister-in-law who were sure to drive him to Bedlam with their antics.

Had it only been this morning that he thought he *might* be in danger? Add that miscalculation to his growing list of things that had been stupidly done.

Richard's eyebrows flew high. "Are you saying that Miss Bingley should be concerned?"

Darcy nodded slowly. He was waist-deep in the rising flood waters of falling in love with Miss Elizabeth, and, at present, he saw no branch to grasp to keep him from being pulled under. "Not that you are to make any comment on that to her or anyone else. It may just be a passing infatuation." He held his cousin's gaze until Richard nodded his acceptance of the demand. "Now, why are you here?"

"Have you forgotten what is in two days?"

Darcy's brow furrowed for a moment. Two days from now would be... November 16. Right. "Are *you* delivering my father's letter?" He had expected it to be sent in the post.

"That I am. I have some time free from duties and volunteered so that I can give you a report about how your sister fares."

"Is she well?"

"Perfectly well. Indeed, she is the best I have seen her in some time. She smiles and laughs. She tolerates father's teasing with aplomb, and Mother says she spends very little time staring sorrowfully off into the distance. And, I suppose, it is good to note that her lessons are progressing well, and she is excelling in most of them. French is still a struggle, but she is eager to please Mrs. Annesley and has been doing more than what is required to speak with the lady in French for an hour a day. It seems that our choice of companion this time was exactly as it should be. We have not failed her."

"This time," Darcy muttered. Her last companion, as it turned out, had been more interested in helping a *friend* secure Georgiana's money than in helping Georgiana prepare for her role in society.

Richard sighed and nodded. "Mrs. Younge was convincing."

That she was. She had said all the right things and had produced glowing letters of recommendation. Darcy was still not sure if those letters were real or forged. He might investigate that some day.

"Her letters were real, save for the dates," Richard continued, as if he was reading Darcy's mind. He was not, of course. Darcy had wondered aloud about those letters more than once. "I did some probing. I needed it settled in my mind as much as you need it settled in yours. We were duped through and through, but we were not tricked by forgery at least."

"I suppose that is something." Not that it actually made Darcy feel any better about letting such a woman have access to his sister.

"I am counting it as such, and I am attempting to put it behind me now. I would suggest you do the same."

That was no small task.

"If Georgie can work at moving forward, so can we." Richard leveled a stern glare at Darcy.

"I am attempting to." Darcy glanced at Netherfield's front door. "Have you greeted Bingley yet?"

Richard shook his head. "I just asked about you and was directed to the garden or the stables by the housekeeper."

"Did you inform her you plan to stay for a few days? You are staying, are you not?"

"I am, and I did, but then, a carriage arrived, so I took myself to the garden. Who was Bingley expecting to call?"

"Miss Elizabeth sent word to her mother to evaluate her sister's condition. I think Miss Bennet would like to go home, but since Miss Elizabeth sent for her mother, I think Miss Elizabeth feels it is too soon for her to travel."

"Are you certain that the mother was not called for because Miss Elizabeth cannot tell how her sister does?"

"No." Darcy chuckled and shook his head. "She is far too intelligent to not know precisely how her sister does, though I suppose she could be attempting to keep Miss Bennet here for Bingley's sake."

"Indeed? Miss Bennet must be beautiful."

Bingley was known for attracting all the prettiest girls.

"She is the personification of the word." Even if she did smile too much.

"And has Bingley lost his heart to her?"

That was a good question, but there was an even better one that poked at Darcy's mind and caused him to worry. "He may have, but I am uncertain if Miss Bennet returns his regard. She is not only pretty but also utterly gracious,

and everyone receives a warm smile of welcome from her."
How was one to determine if the lady was interested in a
gentleman if she treated him no differently than she treated
everyone else? It was most perplexing.

Richard clapped him on the shoulder. "Then, it is
doubly good that I am here, for perhaps I can help you
decipher the truth of the matter."

"I would welcome the assistance." They climbed the
steps and entered Netherfield. "I would like to change
before I break my fast, though it is not entirely necessary,"
Darcy said as he handed his hat to a servant.

"I had hoped to do the same," Richard replied while
removing his gloves. "Unless my trunk has not yet arrived
with my man. Then, I shall just make myself as presentable
as possible on my own." His stomach rumbled. "And
quickly," he added with a laugh.

Chapter 3

ELIZABETH TOOK ONE LAST look at Mr. Darcy as he talked to his cousin when she got to the garden door. That gentleman was an enigma. She had thought she understood his character before their meeting this morning. Now, it appeared she had not known as much about him as she thought she did.

As Mr. Darcy and his cousin began walking in the garden, Elizabeth entered Netherfield and hurried to the entrance hall to greet her mother and... sisters? Why were all her younger sisters with her mother? She sighed inwardly. Was it not possible for her family to show some decorum just once? Being called to the aid of an ill child was not a social call!

However, noting the way Kitty and Lydia were looking around the entrance hall, she supposed it would have been challenging for her mother to leave her most curious, vocal, and favourite daughters at home when they were obviously eager to see Netherfield. But why was Mary here?

"I can take you all to Jane," Elizabeth said after she had kissed her mother's cheek in greeting.

"I do not want to see Jane," Lydia said. "I want to see the ballroom."

Of course, she did! There was little that Lydia liked more than dancing and being seen and doted on.

"Oh, me, too," Kitty said.

That was also not surprising, for it was quite the normal way of things for Kitty to want to do whatever Lydia was doing.

"But I will be happy with just seeing the drawing room," Kitty added. There was a touch of Jane in Kitty.

"We are not here for a tour," Mary chided before turning to Elizabeth. "I will attempt to keep them from embarrassing us too much while you and Mama see to Jane."

Ah, yes, that was the reason Mary had been enlisted to come with their mother – Lydia and Kitty, though mostly Lydia.

"You act as if we are children." Lydia folded her arms and stomped a foot, looking for all the world like a petulant child. "We are not that much younger than you."

"You are not to be introduced until either Elizabeth or I have returned," their mother said before Mary could give

Lydia a proper rejoinder. Scolding her younger sisters was something at which Mary excelled.

"If you will pardon my intrusion," Mrs. Nichols, Netherfield's housekeeper, inserted, "I can see Mrs. Bennet to Miss Bennet's room if that will smooth things a bit."

Elizabeth looked to her mother for a response. Personally, she was torn on what to do. She wanted to see her mother to Jane's room, but she also did not trust her youngest sisters to be left only in Mary's care. Mary would do her best, but a lecture in the entrance hall was not a particularly decorous thing for anyone to witness. It would be bad enough for Mr. Darcy to walk in on such a thing with his cousin. Then, he would not have to look for faults with her family, for they would be presented to him on a platter. But far worse would be for Miss Bingley to happen upon such a scene. She was barely civil to Elizabeth as it was. There was no need to give her more things about which to whisper with her sister, Mrs. Hurst, or insert as veiled criticism in conversation.

"I suppose it will have to do." Mrs. Bennet took Elizabeth by the arm. "However, I would like to have a few words with this daughter before I see my other daughter."

"Of course, ma'am." Mrs. Nichols stepped aside as Mrs. Bennet pulled Elizabeth toward the stairs.

"How do you think Jane fares?" Mrs. Bennet hissed as quietly as she was capable of doing, which to Elizabeth's way of thinking was not quite as quiet as it should be.

"She has a sore throat, a cough, and a fever. She fares ill." Much too ill to be taken outside and required to ride home. Perhaps in a day or two she would be well enough for that, but at present, Elizabeth feared that such activity would deepen the illness and perhaps cause it to become grave.

"No, no, not her health." Mrs. Bennet cast a look towards Mrs. Nichols and lowered her voice even further. "With Mr. Bingley. Will Jane's staying here help him fall in love with her? Or is he, perhaps, already in love with her?" There was a hopeful lilt to Mrs. Bennet's final question.

"Mama, Jane is ill. Her health, not her marital status, should be our concern."

"You may lecture me on what should and should not be my concern when you have five daughters of your own." Her mother gave Elizabeth one of her most severe glares. "Now, about Mr. Bingley."

Elizabeth sighed. It was always about finding a good match with her mother, and Elizabeth supposed she could not fault her completely. It was done out of an abundance of care about her and her sister's futures. Therefore, she pressed the matter no further.

"He is as smitten with her as he ever was, but she worries that she will be a burden. You know how Jane is."

Mrs. Bennet contemplated that for a moment before pursing her lips and lifting her chin. It was a sure sign that she was determined about something and would not be moved.

"There are times," Mrs. Bennet said, "when the unpleasant must be borne to achieve the desired end. If you believe Jane is too ill to travel home, then so do I."

"I did not say that I thought that!" Though, she had thought it. Not that she had thought it just so Mr. Bingley could fall in love with Jane!

"You would not have written to me to come tell Jane she must stay here if you did not think she should not leave. You would have instead enlisted the use of Mr. Bingley's carriage to bring you both home."

Elizabeth opened her mouth to reply but then closed it again without saying a word. It was true. She had only called for their mother to convince Jane that what she said was right.

"The only question which remains is whether Mr. Jones needs to be called for or not." Her mother's lips curled upward, and her eyes sparkled as they did when she was scheming. "Most likely he does. I shall recommend it, I think."

"Mama! Really? Using the apothecary in your matchmaking?"

"Someone must ensure Jane is properly married. She is too retiring to see to it herself." Mrs. Bennet tipped her head to the side and gave Elizabeth an apologetic look. "Unfortunately, that does mean you will need to tolerate Mr. Darcy for a time. Do you think you can do that without causing offense and ruining your sister's chances? Mary said she would be willing to stay if needed."

Tolerating Mr. Darcy would not be too difficult a task after the conversation they had just had in the garden. Elizabeth's interest in him was higher than it had ever been, and not just because he was handsome, as Jane had tried to claim, but because he was intriguing.

"I think I can manage it."

Her mother took her hand and gave it a squeeze. "You are a very generous sister to willingly abide such a rude gentleman on your sister's behalf."

"He apologized." The words were out of Elizabeth's mouth before she could think better of them. As one might expect, her mother's features were instantly suffused with excitement at the news.

"How? What did he say?"

"He said he regretted his words at the assembly." Much like Elizabeth currently regretted having mentioned his apology.

"Is that all?" Mrs. Bennet asked with a tsk. "Did he also apologize for teasing you at Lucas Lodge?"

Elizabeth's cheeks warmed. Yes, she was most certainly regretting mentioning Mr. Darcy's apology, for answering her mother's question honestly was not going to do anything but push forward the idea of a possible match in her mother's mind. "He was not teasing."

Mrs. Bennet's hand flew to her heart. "He was not?"

Elizabeth shook her head. She really needed to learn to not decry supposed insults so heartily. Being wrong was never pleasant, but it was much more unpleasant when the wrong was known by one and all – and most especially when it gave her mother a reason to hope.

"No, he said he truly wanted to dance with me." That still surprised her.

"Oh, you must make him love you. Two daughters married and so handsomely so!"

And there it was. The trouble that would arise from Elizabeth's unguarded words – both in grumbling about Mr. Darcy and in blurting out that he had apologized.

"Mama, I cannot make him love me just because he wanted to dance with me." She was just pleased that he did not seem to despise her as much as she had assumed he had. Indeed, when she had left him moments ago, she had felt like they could possibly, in the future, at some point, be friends.

"Wishing to dance with you is certainly a step in the way of falling in love."

Before Elizabeth could debate the foolishness of such a statement, Netherfield's door opened, and the very gentleman whom her mother wished for her to draw along walked in with his cousin, Colonel Fitzwilliam.

The colonel was not quite so tall and handsome as Mr. Darcy, but he was by no means wanting in appeal. There was something in his carriage and expression that was captivating, and Elizabeth looked forward to making his acquaintance.

"Who is that?" her mother whispered.

"Mr. Darcy's cousin, Colonel Fitzwilliam," Elizabeth replied.

"Have you met him?"

"No, I just know that is who he is because that is who Mr. Darcy said he was."

"Did Mr. Darcy mention if his cousin is married?"

"Mama, Jane is sick. Remember. That is why you are here."

"I am perfectly capable of doing more than one thing at a time, but," she cast a sad eye towards Mr. Darcy and his cousin, "I suppose I shall go to Jane first." She took a step away from Elizabeth, but then returned. "Do you think he looks too old for Lydia?"

"Mama!"

"Then, perhaps, do you think he would be interested in a serious wife like Mary."

"Mama! Go to Jane."

Mrs. Bennet looked ready to leave Elizabeth to find Jane, but before she could, Mr. Darcy crossed the entrance hall to greet her.

"Good day, Mrs. Bennet. I trust being called to check on your daughter has not caused you too much anxiety."

Elizabeth pressed her lips together. Her mother had likely been fluttering about her nerves from the time Elizabeth's message had arrived until she entered the carriage, where she had been required to sit still for the length of time it took to travel the three miles from Longbourn to Netherfield. It was probably then that her nerves had subsided and when she had begun to congratulate herself on her successful scheme in seeing Jane confined to Mr. Bingley's home.

"Oh, not at all. I knew that my Jane was in good hands." She took Elizabeth's hand and lifting it gave it a pat. "Elizabeth is very good at seeing to the wellbeing of her sisters. She is actually quite exceptional at it. Even Lady Lucas says so."

Elizabeth closed her eyes and tried not to feel mortified.

"She does seem to be very devoted to Miss Bennet."

Elizabeth's opened her eyes and met Mr. Darcy's. His smile seemed understanding.

"No truer words could be said, Mr. Darcy, but I should go to Jane anyway." She paused and looked toward the colonel. "And you should see to your guest."

Elizabeth just barely kept her eyes from rolling at the obvious nudge to be introduced.

"May I introduce him to you before you go?" Mr. Darcy asked.

"Indeed, you may," her mother said eagerly.

This time, Elizabeth was a moment too late and did not catch her eye roll until it had happened.

"It will make it easier once we are all settled in the drawing room," Mr. Darcy said to Elizabeth as if he needed to explain his actions to her. Apparently, he had seen her reaction, which was utterly embarrassing.

"Then, our conversation will not need to be interrupted," he continued.

"That seems quite reasonable," was all Elizabeth could think of to say in response. And it was. It was logical. Perfectly logical. As if she expected anything other than a well-thought-out plan from a gentleman like Mr. Darcy.

Chapter 4

"Richard." Mr. Darcy motioned for his cousin to join him. "I thought it best to introduce everyone now since we are all here."

The colonel's lips twitched as if he were attempting not to laugh. "Indeed."

Had he caught the whole interaction? And was he laughing at her or her mother or both?

"This is my cousin, Colonel Richard Fitzwilliam. Cousin, these are Mrs. Bennet, Miss Elizabeth Bennet, Miss Mary Bennet, Miss Kitty Bennet, and Miss Lydia Bennet."

"I have come to see my eldest, Jane. She is sick," Mrs. Bennet added.

"I am sorry to hear that. I trust her illness is nothing of a grave nature."

"Oh, no. I am certain it is not, and she has been in good care."

"Mr. Bingley is a most solicitous host," Elizabeth inserted before her mother could once again expound on Elizabeth's excellence when it came to nursing the sick back to health. Truly, she was no better at it than any other lady who had half a care to see to the wellbeing of another.

"I am delighted to hear that," Mr. Bingley said as he descended the stairs in front of which they were all gathered.

"Mrs. Bennet." He took her hand. "Do let me know if I should send for the apothecary."

"I think it would be best. I am surprised Elizabeth has not already done so. She really is excellent at knowing when such things must be done, but I suppose she wished to defer to her mother as any dutiful daughter would." She peeked at Mr. Darcy.

"I think you should see Jane before you decide." Elizabeth gave her mother a small nudge toward the stairs.

"I suppose you are correct, but I dare say I will only see what you do."

"I will have a footman ready to fetch Mr. Jones when your assessment is done," Mr. Bingley said. "In the meantime, while we wait to hear Mrs. Bennet's evaluation of your sister's need for the apothecary, have you ladies broken your fast?"

"We would not wish to impose," Mary answered.

"It is not an imposition at all." Mr. Bingley assured her. "Colonel, have you eaten?"

"Not since very early this morning before I began my ride to Netherfield."

"Well, then, I suggest that we all retire to the morning room *tout de suite* and find some sustenance, unless you gentlemen wish to change or refresh yourselves first?"

Mr. Darcy looked to the colonel, who shook his head. "It seems it can wait."

Looking quite satisfied by that reply, Mr. Bingley turned to Mrs. Bennet. "I can have something sent up to you and Miss Bennet. Do not be shy in making your wishes known."

Elizabeth had to bite her lip to keep from laughing. Her mother was anything but reluctant about making her desires known. Colonel Fitzwilliam caught her eye and winked. Heat raced across Elizabeth's cheeks. Was he making fun of her mother? He would not be the first, but most were not so blatantly obvious about it.

"What mother is shy about making her wishes known?" he whispered to her while Mrs. Bennet was taking her leave and Mr. Bingley was restating his desire to see to both her and Jane's care. "Mine is not," he added.

So, it was a shared burden and not a mocking of her mother, was it? "And what are your mother's wishes for you, sir?"

"That I would refrain from ruining either myself or my uniform by allowing a bullet to hit me, and that, at some point, I would make her happy and choose to follow my father into politics, for when I do, she thinks I will then take a wife and produce grandchildren for her."

"Oh." That was rather to the point. Refreshingly so. Perhaps, he was not the mocking sort.

"I cannot say that her desires are not slowly becoming my own. However, you are never to tell her that," he added conspiratorially.

Elizabeth laughed. "I shall not reveal your secret unless necessary." She placed her hand on the colonel's proffered arm.

"And why would it ever become necessary?"

"I could not rightly tell you, but one must not concede advantages unnecessarily, even if one does not know when one might need them."

The colonel chuckled. "That is well said, Miss Elizabeth."

"I try my best not to be ill-spoken. I find being well-spoken to be so much better," Elizabeth teased.

The colonel once again chuckled as together they followed Mr. Bingley and Mr. Darcy into the small, sun-filled morning room that was laid out for breakfast.

"There will be more of us than normal," Mr. Bingley said to one of the footmen who stood near a sideboard that held a great number of covered dishes. "And Mrs. Bennet and Miss Bennet will require a tray taken above stairs."

"Right away, sir."

"Oh, and someone should be ready to fetch Mr. Jones if needed," Bingley added before the footman left the room. Then, he turned to his guests. "Do indulge yourselves as little or as much as you would like."

Shortly after, as everyone was gathering their food and finding a place to sit, another footman entered with more dishes.

"Oh, my!" Miss Bingley said as she entered the room just after the footman had. "I had no idea we were having a dinner party so early in the day." She gave her brother a pointed look.

"It is a breakfast party, my dear sister," he replied with a smile. "A dinner party in the morning would be quite ridiculous. Do you not agree, Miss Lydia?"

"Oh, indeed!" Lydia assured him while Kitty giggled.

"Are Louisa and Hurst joining us?" Mr. Bingley continued as if nothing at all had happened.

"They will join us later," Miss Bingley said. "Which appears to be an excellent thing, since we are already so many."

"I could not agree more."

Mr. Bingley's smile had not faltered once in the whole exchange. In Elizabeth's mind, his ability to tolerate his sisters and his brother-in-law, Mr. Hurst, spoke well to his being able to tolerate her family should he marry Jane, which she hoped he did. She had never seen Jane so enamoured with any gentleman before. There was only one problem with the whole situation.

"A penny for your thoughts?" Colonel Fitzwilliam interrupted Elizabeth's ruminations.

Elizabeth shook her head.

"Please? The crown trusts me with secrets, so surely you can, too."

"I fear it will not show me in a good light."

"Ah!" he said as if he could read her mind. "Are you thinking that you wish to be rid of Miss Bingley?"

A startled burst of laughter escaped Elizabeth. "No."

"I am," he said with another wink.

The man was both forward and a bit of a flirt.

"Very well, I was thinking something like that. Do you think your cousin would possibly be willing to marry her?"

Next to her, the colonel nearly choked on his tea. "My cousin?" He shook his head. "Why?"

"It would make things more bearable for Jane," Elizabeth admitted in a whisper.

"Do your sister's affections lie with Mr. Bingley then?"

"Do not tell her I said so."

"I will not say a word unless necessary."

Elizabeth held his gaze. "And if sharing such a secret becomes necessary for you, then, I shall be forced to reveal your secret to your mother."

The colonel laughed heartily at that.

"What is so hilarious?" Miss Bingley's tone was sharp.

"Nothing of importance," the colonel replied. "You have provided a most delightful array of foods, Miss Bingley."

Miss Bingley's chin lifted. It was an action she seemed to favour, as it likely made it easier for her to look down her nose at others. Elizabeth had seen her affect that air of superiority several times since arriving at Netherfield.

"As if there is any other way to do it." Miss Bingley cut a sly, hopeful glance toward Mr. Darcy who was seated on the other side of his cousin and next to Mr. Bingley. That was another thing she was always doing – looking for Mr. Darcy's approval.

Elizabeth looked at the colonel who shook his head and whispered, "Sadly, no."

"Are you certain?"

Colonel Fitzwilliam chuckled. "Yes, very."

Well, that was too bad. How was she supposed to help her sister find a happy future if she could not rid Mr. Bingley of his unmarried sister? It was a conundrum and one which she likely would not be able to solve.

Mary, who was seated next to her, gave her a nudge. "About what are you talking?"

Elizabeth gave her sister a small shake of her head. This was not the place or time to discuss the problem of Miss Bingley with anyone.

"Will you tell me later?" Mary whispered.

Elizabeth nodded. "But not Lydia and Kitty."

"I would not even think of sharing it with them. Especially not today." This was said with a frustrated huff and a roll of Mary's eyes. "I was supposed to practice the piano this morning, but because of them, I had to get dressed and come here to be looked at with disdain by Miss Bingley."

"She is rather all about herself, is she not?" Elizabeth agreed.

"Excessively so. How have you managed being here? All day? Every day?"

"I have spent a great deal of my time with Jane." She leaned a little closer to Mary. "Even while Jane was sleeping, since the conversation was guaranteed to be better."

Mary chuckled.

"I feel left out," the colonel said. "Miss Mary, is it?"

Mary nodded and smiled as she simultaneously tucked the right corner of her lower lip between her teeth as if attempting to limit the spread of her happiness at being spoken to by the colonel.

Elizabeth could not fault her for being enamoured with a gentleman such as the colonel. There really was just something charming about the man.

"This room is very bright." Lydia voice cut through the moment of quiet conversation that might have arisen between Elizabeth, Mary, and the colonel. "I think it is the brightest morning room I have ever seen."

"Netherfield is not without its charms," Miss Bingley said with another sideward glance at Mr. Darcy.

"Oh, indeed, it is not!" Lydia cried as Elizabeth wondered if Miss Bingley would find Netherfield so charming if Mr. Darcy were not in residence.

"I have always wondered how it looked inside," Lydia continued. I have always thought it was lovely from the outside, and I believe it is nearly as large as Longbourn. Would you not agree, Kitty?"

"I would indeed, but I do think that it might be the way the rooms are arranged that make it seem that way, if it is not actually that way."

"What do you mean?" Lydia asked.

"Netherfield is much more modern and has rooms stacked upon rooms as all the newer homes do, you know," Kitty answered. "Longbourn is old and rambling with bits and pieces added here and there. Mind you, it is all very nicely done, like a lovely little rabbit's warren," she added. "But it is not the modern way of doing things."

"There have been homes with many floors and those with rambling halls and corridors for years," Mary's tone carried some of the irritation that Elizabeth knew she must be feeling towards her younger sisters for their interference with her plans for the day. "I would not say that building a house with several floors is new."

"But Netherfield is new when you compare it to our home," Kitty insisted.

"You are not always right," Lydia muttered with a glare for Mary.

Elizabeth drew a deep breath and hoped that a true argument would not begin between her sisters. Thankfully, the possibility of a row was put to an end by the colonel.

"I think you are both correct," he inserted into the conversation. "There have been tall houses for years, but one must agree after seeing several newer builds that the taller house seems to be a la mode even when the halls and corridors ramble across the landscape."

"It is truly the way in which a home is presented that is of importance, not the age. A house can be recently built and yet, through neglect, the gardens can become overgrown and the interior can be tattered and dreadful." Miss Bingley lifted her cup of tea. "Of course, a proper mistress of her home would not allow for such a thing to happen."

"Unless she marries a miscreant," the colonel replied. "Then, her task will be much more challenging."

"Proper ladies do not marry miscreants. They do not even entertain them as suitors." Miss Bingley took another sip of her tea.

"Well, I do not wish to marry a bore, but I do want a beautiful home," Lydia said.

Mr. Bingley laughed. "I think there are some of us gentlemen who are neither bores nor troublemakers, Miss Lydia."

"As you get older, that will become more evident." Miss Bingley hid a mocking smile behind her teacup.

"We all learn better about the world and how to walk in it as we age." Mr. Darcy directed a pointed look at Miss Bingley before sending a friendly smile towards Miss Lydia. "My sister is about your age, and she is finding there is still much she does not know. As am I."

"Hear, hear," Colonel Fitzwilliam agreed heartily. "Improving one's understanding of things should never end."

"Never?" Lydia asked with no small amount of surprise and more than a touch of horror. Lydia was not fond of learning, so Elizabeth imagined the thought of it never being over was not a welcome one for her.

"Never," Mary replied before stealing a surreptitious look at the colonel.

Elizabeth picked up her teacup and cradled it in her hands as she reclined in her chair and sighed silently.

Sisters: those who were curious and unable to hold their tongues, those who were mean, though not her own, those who were dear and unwell, and those who seemed willing to easily have their hearts touched.

How was she supposed to navigate through this sea of sisters and keep her dignity while attempting to keep those hearts she loved most in all the world from being injured?

She looked behind the colonel to Mr. Darcy. How did he manage it? True, he only had one sister, but perhaps he had some advice? Maybe she would ask him now that he seemed a bit more like a friend than a foe.

Chapter 5

DARCY LOOKED UP FROM his book. He had been attempting to read the same page for the past quarter hour, but it was no use. His mind was much more interested in the lady standing near the window than in whatever was written on a dusty old page of a novel.

Well, actually, it was not an old or dusty page. In reality, it was quite new. Recently published, even. And the story bound within this volume of paper, ink, and leather about a wife and daughters being turned out of their home by a weak-minded man and his money-grubbing wife did not lack interest.

It was just that no amount of Dashwood ladies and lost estates could captivate Darcy the way Miss Elizabeth did as she stood at the window, looking out at Netherfield Park's gardens. It was where she had been standing since before he and Richard had entered the room.

Her head tipped from side to side, slowly, as if stretching her neck. Then, as if to prove his supposition correct, she rubbed the right side of her lovely neck. Her shoulders lifted and lowered noticeably. She seemed tired. He hoped she was not going to fall ill herself from not getting enough rest while caring for her sister.

Richard's boot bumped Darcy's foot, drawing his attention away from the pleasant prospect of Miss Elizabeth. His cousin's grin made him shake his head before turning his attention back to his book, though to be honest, his eyes still wandered to Miss Elizabeth nearly every other word.

Next to Darcy, while he was attending to his book in a very inattentive fashion, Richard shuffled the papers he was reading. They contained some information about his inheritance and his commission in the regulars. Surprisingly, he had not been teasing when he had told Miss Elizabeth yesterday that he was contemplating fulfilling his mother's wishes.

Darcy cast a surreptitious glance in his cousin's direction and saw him wince as he shifted position and stretched his right leg out in front of him. That was the leg which had both caught a bullet and been broken when falling from his horse about a year ago. That event had occurred just shortly before Richard had begun listening to his mother's suggestions about what he should do with his life without as many counterarguments as had been his normal wont.

Movement at the window as Miss Elizabeth turned from it caught Darcy's attention again. As he turned an unread page in his book, she returned to her seat and took up the needlework she had discarded on the table next to her chair. It was well-done from what Darcy could see, and he had spent several minutes examining it from a distance when he was not looking at her. She was most certainly not a lady without accomplishments.

"How is Miss Bennet this morning?" he asked.

The object of so many of his thoughts lately looked up from her stitching and smiled at him. Hers was an excessively charming smile that made her eyes sparkle.

"Her fever is substantially lower, and I believe she had a restful night's sleep. Calling the apothecary was the correct thing to do."

Mrs. Bennet had declared Mr. Jones needed to be summoned when she had joined them in the drawing room yesterday, and Bingley had been only too happy to lend his aid. Darcy's friend was clearly smitten with Miss Bennet.

"I am happy to hear that she is improving."

"If her improvement continues as it has been since last night, she might be able to leave her room this evening for a time." She sighed.

Darcy knew that sound. It was the one that he often made when worried about his own sister.

"And," Miss Elizabeth continued, "that should help me evaluate how soon we will be able to travel home."

"Is your sister still anxious to leave Netherfield?"

"She is." Miss Elizabeth's gaze lowered from meeting his to looking at the work in her lap. "Though, perhaps, she is not as anxious as I am to be home." She gave a small shrug but did not look up.

"Are you anxious to leave us?" This news surprised Darcy, though it probably should not.

Caroline had done her utmost to be haughty and off-putting yesterday after the other Miss Bennets and their mother had left. She had not even attempted to keep her disparaging words about the Bennets from being heard by Miss Elizabeth. In fact, Darcy was nearly certain she had intended for Miss Elizabeth to be humiliated.

Even Bingley had grown short-tempered with her and had taken her to task over it after Miss Elizabeth had disappeared to check on her sister.

Miss Elizabeth had never returned to the drawing room.

That lady drew a deep breath and looked up at him and Richard. "I am an imposition."

"Only to Miss Bingley," Richard said.

"And Mrs. Hurst," Miss Elizabeth added.

Louisa had been nearly as caustic as her younger sister, Caroline, last night. The discomfort Darcy had felt on Miss Elizabeth's behalf then, now grew into true sorrow at the sadness in her expression.

"I do not wish to make things more difficult for my sister." She shifted her gaze to something beyond Darcy's shoulder and sat quietly for a moment before asking, "How do you do it?" Her eyes met his eyes once again.

"Do what?"

"Care completely for the welfare of a sister and remain..." Her eyes scanned Darcy's face as she searched for a word. "Placid?"

A bark of laugher escaped Richard, and Darcy could understand why. He was the furthest thing from placid when it came to making any decision about his sister. He questioned everything he did for her. It was how his temperament was. However, his agitation about such things had increased ever since the incident in Ramsgate in the summer.

"I do not see to her care completely. At present, my sister is at home in the care of a companion, and then, there are also my aunt and uncle, as well as my cousin," he glanced at Richard, "who help me. In fact, her guardianship is not even my sole responsibility."

Her brow furrowed. "It is not?"

He shook his head. "Richard is also Georgiana's guardian."

Miss Elizabeth's lovely eyes grew wide as she looked between him and his cousin. "Both of you?"

"We are more like brothers than cousins," Richard said. "We always have been."

He shifted positions again, this time without a trace of discomfort. "This way, with both Darcy and I as guardians, both sides of Darcy's family feel included in the life of his sister, and that placates most of our relations. At least, somewhat. Lady Catherine will always be Lady Catherine, and she is rarely mollified."

"I see."

Miss Elizabeth's brow furrowed, and Darcy wondered if she did, in fact, understand or not.

"You were both very young to take on such a responsibility, were you not?" she asked Richard.

"Indeed, we were. I am only one year older than Darcy, and he will be twenty-eight three months from tomorrow. That is, as a matter of fact, why I am here."

The letters. Darcy sighed. They were weighing heavily on him today, and he had Caroline to thank for the greater share of that.

"I am grieved that Miss Bingley and Mrs. Hurst have caused you to be uneasy," Darcy said to Miss Elizabeth. And he was. He had never been so disgusted with Caroline as he had been last night. Her behaviour had shone a glaringly bright light on his own poor behaviour, and he knew of only one appropriate way to deal with it. "I have not been the sort of man my father would have wanted for me to be, and, for that, I apologize."

Confusion suffused Miss Elizabeth's features.

"What do you mean?" Richard looked just as puzzled as Miss Elizabeth.

"I have been less than gracious about Bingley's neighbours." He shook his head. That was putting things gently. "As is my tradition before receiving the new missive Father left for me, I reread the ones I have already received. I read them last night." It had been like sitting in his father's study receiving a lecture after having committed a grievous sin.

"Tomorrow's is the last," Richard said.

Darcy nodded. "I know. I wish it was not."

His father's letters had been a balm to his soul this past year and would remain with him for as long as was humanly possible just so he could open them and hear his father speak to him – even if those words were a reproof such as he had received from them last night.

Richard reached over and laid his hand on Darcy's shoulder briefly. It was a small gesture of understanding and comfort. His cousin was one of the few who were privy to just how greatly Darcy missed and longed for his father's guidance.

"In reading those letters," Darcy continued. "I was reminded of what he has always taught me. He would not be pleased with my attitude about being here – not even if I have a good reason for being ill-humored."

"What letters?" Miss Elizabeth asked softly, almost as if she were afraid to intrude upon a private conversation or ask something which might cause another to be injured when providing an answer.

"Before my father died, when he knew he was ill and would not recover, he spent a great deal of time teaching me everything he could to prepare me to assume the running of Pemberley. He had always taught me things. My education was not lacking, but his teaching and reteaching took on a sense of desperation. It was as if he wanted to put an additional twenty-three years of life together into our relationship in those last few months."

Her lips parted as if she was going to speak, but then, she pressed them together.

"I know that does not answer your question," Darcy replied with a smile. "Along with pouring what remained of his strength into preparing me to take up my role as master of a grand estate, and completely unbeknownst to me, he wrote four letters which contain final instructions and reminders. These letters were to be given to me during my twenty-seventh year of life – one on each quarter day beginning with my birthday and ending tomorrow."

"Oh, that is a lovely gift." Miss Elizabeth's eyes glistened with tears that spoke to how deeply she understood the significance of the letters Darcy had received from his father.

"It is a bittersweet gift, to be honest," Darcy said.

"Do you still miss him greatly?"

"Though it has been five years, I do. At some times more than others, of course."

Like this past summer. He was certain his father would have never hired a companion for Georgiana who would prove to be untrustworthy.

And now, when he had found a lady that spoke to his heart. If only his father were alive to counsel him on the wisdom of letting his heart rule his head on this.

Chapter 6

MISS ELIZABETH PICKED UP her stitching and then, put it back in her lap. "May I ask something about the letters?"

"Certainly."

"Why did you have to wait so long to receive them?"

It was a good question and one which Darcy had asked when his uncle, Richard's father, had given him the first letter.

"It is because Georgiana will be presented to society next year. There are two purposes to my father's wish to delay my receiving the letters. Firstly, he wanted to remind me of everything he had taught me, and secondly, he wanted to prepare me for the task of seeing my sister well-settled when the time comes to trust some gentleman with the responsibility of being her husband. The first letter explained his reason and instructed me about the importance of family – my sister, in particular. I have seen and am seeing to her preparation to be presented as best I am able to do. With Richard's help, of course."

"And the help of a proper companion." Richard gave Darcy a significant look. It was one that told him to stop doubting himself as to how well he was caring for his sister.

"Yes, and with the help of a companion. The second letter was about seeing to my estate." He chuckled. "My father would have probably liked to have written a dozen or more letters about that topic. He was an excellent manager of Pemberley. I was fortunate to inherit an estate that is in such good order, and I have worked to keep it that way and to improve upon it, since he was particularly insistent that I should not think about Pemberley as remaining as it has always been. He was always looking to the future and preparing for it, and he encouraged me to do the same."

"I think that is the best way to think," Elizabeth said with a light laugh. "One should not root oneself too firmly to what has always been. One should learn from it, but not cling to it as if it is the only way things can be."

"My uncle would have agreed with that sentiment exactly," Richard said.

"Indeed, he would have," Darcy agreed. "Father said things very similar to that quite often."

"Often enough that even I heard them." Richard laughed. "And I was not the one receiving instruction."

"It sounds like you had an excellent father." Her expression was soft and filled with delight. She was not merely saying words. She was, in this moment, expressing her true, unguarded feelings, and Darcy dared to hope that their tentative friendship was growing into something more settled.

"I did. He was not perfect, but he was a good man." And Darcy knew that he would not go wrong if he followed much of his father's example. "I hope to one day be as good a father as he was."

"Or better." Richard winked at Elizabeth, who laughed.

"In some way, perhaps," Darcy admitted.

"Would it be terribly forward of me to ask what the third letter was about?" Miss Elizabeth tucked a corner of her lower lip between her teeth and gave him the most charmingly uncertain look he had ever seen. How had he declared her not tempting enough for him? There truly were moments when he was an utter idiot.

Richard cleared his throat.

"Oh, no, it is perfectly reasonable to ask as I have been open in sharing about the other letters." Heat climbed up his neck at having been caught admiring Miss Elizabeth.

"In fact, it is that third letter that has scolded me quite soundly, for it is about friendship and one's place in one's own society. I have not been respectful and gracious. I have not set aside my preferences to allow for the foibles of others. I have not welcomed new surroundings nor wished myself to be welcomed in them. In plain terms, I have been self-indulgent and arrogant. In this, I have failed my father the most. It would not matter to him that my failure happened when I was attempting to do as he instructed, he would still be altogether disappointed in my behaviour.

"While I came to Netherfield to lend my aid to a friend and help guide him in making a decision of no small significance – which is all well and good, commendable even – I did not want to come. I wanted to stay at home in London with my sister."

He glanced at Richard. "Before I came to Hertfordshire, I thought that I had failed my father most severely, but that misstep was merely a poor decision with tragic results that I could not have controlled, for I had been duped. This, however? This was a willful refusal to put aside my displeasure at doing what I did not want to do. Unlike the previous incident, my behaviour since arriving at Netherfield has been completely under my command."

"Georgiana was nearly lost to us this past summer," Richard inserted.

Miss Elizabeth gasped, and her eyes grew wide.

"It was the work of a charlatan who pretended to love her, and it is why Darcy did not want to leave her and come here," Richard continued. "This is not general knowledge, but knowing how dearly you care for your sister, I do not fear telling you this much."

Her eyes flicked from Richard to Darcy and back to Richard. "Oh, of course, not a word will be shared."

"The scheme was discovered in time to prevent the worst," Darcy said. Losing Georgiana to a former friend who only loved her money would have been devastating, to put it mildly. "Of course, there was damage done. Georgie's heart is healing, but it is scarred." Likely for life. It was such a soft and gentle heart. How could it not be permanently marred?

Miss Elizabeth sat silently looking at him with her right hand resting on her heart. "Well, then," she finally said, "I suppose I have my answer about how we care for sisters. We cannot do more than our best, and even when we are doing our best, we cannot keep them completely from harm."

"Hear, hear. We are not God. Our powers are limited," Richard agreed.

Darcy would do well to remember that. He could not control all things, no matter how much he wished to.

"Thank you," Miss Elizabeth said with a smile for Darcy and then Richard. "You have eased my mind somewhat."

Darcy blinked. "By exposing my faults?" How could his failure make her feel better about her situation with her sisters?

"Precisely."

"How so?"

She lifted her right shoulder and let it fall in a half-shrug. "You strike me, for the most part, to be an intelligent gentleman." Her lips twitched with barely contained amusement.

"For the most part?" Darcy arched an eyebrow.

"There was that comment at the assembly." She held his gaze.

He shook his head. "I did apologize for that."

"Oh, indeed, you did, but that does not erase it from ever having happened."

"Does not forgiveness require you to not lay my sins before me?"

This time, when her lips twitched, amusement won, and she laughed. "You sound very much like my sister Mary."

Richard chuckled. "Miss Mary did seem to be the serious sort. Not that I am disparaging that."

"It is not as if Mary is incapable of fun and frivolity." Miss Elizabeth paused, and her brow furrowed as her face scrunched in thought. "I suppose even in that she is serious." She sighed.

"And that worries you?" Darcy asked.

She nodded. "But that is for another time. At present, I am explaining that your faults have eased my mind because if someone like you, who is intelligent and caring – a fact that I have based on your willingness to help Mr. Bingley and to be so affected by your faults as you are – and who is so actively involved in doing his duty..." Here she paused as if she wanted to say more but dared not. "Unlike some," she said with a weak smile.

Was she thinking of her own father?

"If you cannot prevent all ill from befalling your sister, then, who am I to think I can? Therefore, I must strive to be satisfied with my best effort and not perfection." She heaved a deep sigh. "Not that the thought sits easily, mind you."

Richard laughed. "No, that thought never sits lightly, does it, Darcy?"

"No, it does not." Missing the mark of perfection often pushed him towards ill humour.

Miss Elizabeth picked up her stitching. "What do you think the final letter will be about?"

Darcy shook his head. "I could not even venture a guess."

"He will know tomorrow." Richard tossed a teasing grin at Darcy. "Maybe, Miss Elizabeth, if you decide to brave the barbs of Miss Bingley until Tuesday, which is when your mother said she thought your sister would be well enough to travel, we will both be able to discover what the topic of that letter is."

"It might not be something which can be shared," she replied.

"Will you stay anyway?" Darcy surprised himself with the question as much as he seemed to have startled Miss Elizabeth with it. "We have only just begun to be friends." That sounded like a good reason for why he wanted her to stay. And by good reason, he meant one that he could accept with any amount of equanimity.

"I am not certain that staying is in my sister's best interest, but..." That corner of her lower lip was once again tucked between her teeth. She seemed torn between two options that called to her in equal measure.

"I think it might be in Miss Bennet's best interest," Richard whispered. "I have known Bingley for nearly as long as Darcy has. Your mother's wishes could be more easily attained if you stay."

"Do you truly think so? Does he admire her?" There was a pronounced note of hope in Miss Elizabeth's tone.

It appeared that Darcy's fear about his friend's feelings not being returned was just as unfounded as Richard had declared it to be last night in the billiards room while they waited for Bingley to complete his task of scolding his sister.

"He is smitten," Richard continued, "and as I always say, strike when there is an opening that promises success."

Miss Elizabeth shifted her eyes from Richard to Darcy. "I am not sure if I should."

Darcy bit his tongue to keep from begging her to stay. There was being friendly, and then, there was pathetic. Begging would be pathetic, and it would do nothing to settle his mind where the lovely Miss Elizabeth was concerned. As it was, his need to forcefully restrain himself from pleading with her to stay was doing a fine job of causing his mind to twist and turn in confusion.

"We cannot make your decision for you," Richard said when Darcy remained quiet. "But what harm could there be in being cautious about moving your sister too soon?"

Her brow furrowed. "I suppose I can put off making a decision about when would be best for Jane to travel until she has been in company twice with out ill-effect?" Her uncertainty lifted the end of her sentence, turning it into a question.

Darcy finally allowed his tongue to move to give her an answer. "That might be best," he assured her. Even if it was not best, it most certainly, and rather disturbingly, made him feel at peace to know that he would not lose her company just yet.

Chapter 7

ELIZABETH OPENED THE CURTAINS in the room she was sharing with Jane and let the sun spill across the floor and wrap itself around the furniture. "It looks like it is going to be another beautiful day. I suppose we will have rain soon. It is not as if fine days can continue forever."

She crossed the room, sat on the edge of Jane's bed, and took her sister's hand. "How are you?"

Jane turned her face away from Elizabeth and coughed lightly before answering. "I think I feel well enough to go home."

Elizabeth sighed. "Are you truly in a rush to leave Mr. Bingley? You have just now become well enough to visit with him."

"I was here to attend a dinner and have been required to remain for so long. It is not what the staff expected, and what about Mr. Bingley's budget?"

"Mr. Bingley is not Papa. I am quite certain he has not grumbled in jest or truth about having two more mouths to feed." She rubbed Jane's hand between hers. "You have barely required anything from any of his servants. You are quite the model guest if there ever was one. Come, tell me. What is your real reason for still wishing to go home before you are well and Mama has agreed you can travel?"

There had to be some reason for her sister's continued demand to leave. While it was like Jane to not wish to be a burden on anyone, it was not like her to continue to press an issue after being denied her desire more than once – especially if one of those denials had come from one of their parents.

"It is not right that you should have to be subjected to Mr. Darcy." There was almost a note of question in her voice, as if she were checking to see if Elizabeth would believe her reason.

"I have already told you that he apologized and has become a friend. I do not mind having to be in company with him." Indeed, she quite liked it. "You will have to try again if you wish to convince me that you need to leave."

Jane heaved a great sigh that was punctuated by another shallow cough. "Mr. Bingley is not unattached." She pulled her hand from Elizabeth's and ran both of her hands back and forth along the edge of the coverlet as she spoke. "I must leave before my heart cannot bear the pain of pushing him away."

Elizabeth blinked. "What?"

Jane lifted tear-filled eyes to Elizabeth. "I fear I love him, and it is too late to not be injured, but I cannot tear him away from another."

"I am still confused. What do you mean he is 'not unattached'? You cannot mean that there is someone other than you who holds his affections. It is simply too impossible to consider. I absolutely cannot think that his is a character that could be duplicitous, and since he is clearly smitten with you – both Mr. Darcy and Colonel Fitzwilliam say he is – there can be no other!"

"Then, I must leave immediately!" Jane cried as she pushed back the covers. "I will walk home if I must." She wrapped her arms around herself as she shivered while slipping her feet over the edge of the bed.

"You will not walk home, nor will you be out of bed for very long. You are cold in a room that is quite warm." Elizabeth had moved around the bed to where Jane sat putting on her slippers. She sat next to her and wrapped an arm around her. "To whom do you believe Mr. Bingley is promised?"

"Miss Darcy," Jane whispered. "Caroline and Louisa could not stop talking about her all through dinner. I did not know what to say. I felt so inferior to Miss Darcy. She has had all the best training. She has an uncle who is an earl, and her dowry is thirty thousand pounds! She is everything that someone as good as Mr. Bingley should have as a wife."

"She is Lydia's age."

Jane stilled. "She is?"

"And she is not out."

"She is not?"

"No. Mr. Darcy said so, and..." How could she say what she knew about Miss Darcy only recently being disappointed in love without breaking her promise to Mr. Darcy? She could not think of a way. "And I do not think Mr. Darcy would be quite so serene about his friend being smitten with you if his sister's heart was in danger of being broken."

"I suppose that is true."

"I *know* it is true. And the colonel is also Miss Darcy's guardian. Do you think he would allow Mr. Bingley to pay court to you when his charge is promised to him?"

"I suppose not."

"I *know* he would not."

"Then, why would Caroline and Louisa talk like Miss Darcy was soon to be their sister?" Jane rose from the bed and went behind the screen where the wash basin stood.

"Because they would like it to be true."

Jane poked her head out from behind the screen. "Enough to lie about it?"

Elizabeth sighed. Jane could be far too willing to see the best in everyone. "Miss Bingley and Mrs. Hurst are not good and kind like you. I have not said anything because I did not want to give you any other reason to feel uncomfortable about staying, but both of them have been horrid. Neither are happy to be in Hertfordshire. Apparently, there is nowhere on earth that can compare to the pleasures of London except for Pemberley."

"Have they said so?"

"Several times and in several different ways. The roads are far too dusty. The fields are small. The hills are merely inconvenient bumps that obstruct the view. If only Hertfordshire were as beautiful as Derbyshire, they would be far more content to spend their time here, but according to them, it is quite trite really."

"Hertfordshire is not commonplace," Jane protested. "It is lovely. I have never seen anything in town that is as pretty as a Hertfordshire sunrise or sunset, and I have seen some beautiful things while in town with Aunt and Uncle Gardiner." Jane's chemise flopped over the top of the screen. "Ballrooms in London might sparkle far more than our assembly room, but they are so much less friendly, and that is what the true beauty of an assembly is – the atmosphere of friends and fun."

Jane was definitely feeling better if she could launch such an impassioned defence of the assembly room in Meryton, which was not in disrepair but was in want of some improvements and modernizations.

"What Miss Bingley and Mrs. Hurst have said about Hertfordshire pales in comparison with what they have hinted at about our mother and sisters."

Jane, who was half-dressed, stepped out from behind the screen and looked at Elizabeth in shock. "Have they said unkind things about our family?"

Elizabeth nodded.

"Like what?" Jane demanded as Elizabeth began helping her with her day dress.

"I do not want to distress you more. You are not well enough to bear it."

"I will bear it just fine," Jane snapped.

Elizabeth chuckled silently. Jane was all that was pleasant and calm until she was pushed past what she could tolerate. Once you passed that boundary, there would be a price to pay.

"Remember, I am not saying this. I am only repeating it," Elizabeth cautioned.

"Just tell me."

"During a conversation on Thursday night, Mrs. Hurst said, 'Are you not glad you were never so naïve as the youngest Miss Bennets?' To which, Miss Bingley replied, 'Oh, I never could have been so lacking in sense. We had the best governess Papa could afford, and besides that, *our mother* was intelligent.'"

That was the last of the conversation Elizabeth had stayed below stairs to hear that evening. After that, and before she could say something which might cause Jane further trouble with such cruel future relations, she had taken herself and her book to bed, here in this room, on the cot in the corner, where she had read for a while, but not until after she had given Miss Bingley and Mrs. Hurst a thorough and scathing mental scolding. It had been all she could do to keep from watering her pillow with tears of anger, frustration, and hurt.

Jane stood silently for a full minute before replying. When she did, it was with a perfectly lovely smile – a too perfectly lovely smile. "I wonder then, how she will feel when our *unintelligent* mother and *silly* sisters are her relations?"

She turned toward the dressing table. "I believe that I will take my breakfast downstairs. I have yet to have a good conversation with Mr. Darcy and his cousin. I understand that Mr. Darcy has a sister whom I would dearly like to hear all about." Her pleasant smile turned sly as she sat to let Elizabeth fix her hair. "Especially since I understand she will perhaps be our neighbour once she and Mr. Bingley marry."

"Are you truly going to tell Mr. Darcy that?" With all her heart, Elizabeth hoped she did.

"I will not say anything that is not true according to what Caroline and Louisa have said to me. I will simply let their words form their own noose."

Elizabeth hugged her sister from behind. "Are we staying?"

"I definitely think it is best." Jane's lashes fluttered over a not-so-innocent look. "I am not as well as one might think. I will take breakfast, during which I will have a conversation, and then, I will return to my room to rest so that –"

A tapping at the door interrupted Jane.

"Mr. Bingley wished to know if Miss Bennet needed a tray brought to her this morning," a maid said when Elizabeth opened the door.

"Is he at breakfast?" Jane asked.

"He is indeed, with the colonel and Mr. Darcy."

"Will you tell him that my sister will join him in five minutes because she thinks she is strong enough to venture from her room for a short time?" Elizabeth said.

The maid smiled broadly. "I can, and may I say, Miss Bennet, that I am happy to hear you are doing better? We have all been worried about you – me and the other maids. My mum is a particular friend of Mrs. Hill."

"Thank you. I am very pleased to be doing better. I am certain I will need a rest after I have eaten, but it is wonderful to be able to be in company even for a short time."

"I am sure it is," the maid said before curtseying and scurrying away.

"Yes, the servants have been so put upon by your being here." Elizabeth's tone dripped with sarcasm.

"That was one maid, not every servant. She may not speak for the cook or the footman who had to go fetch Mr. Jones." She took the brush from Elizabeth. "I think I will leave my hair down except for a few pieces being put up. I will just have to redo it once I lie down."

"Yes, I am sure your decision has nothing to do with what Mama has said about flowing hair and how it makes a gentleman's fingers itch to touch it."

Jane shrugged. "Has Mama said that?" She pressed her lips together to keep from laughing. This playful side of Jane was one that was tucked away and rarely seen outside of the private family rooms at Longbourn.

"I will pin your hair partially up but only if you promise me that you are doing this because you have lost your heart to Mr. Bingley and not just to spite his sisters."

Jane laughed. "I have enough troublesome sisters. I have no need to add two more without gaining some blessing in the process."

"Do you love him, then?"

"I think I do." Her brow furrowed. "No, I do not think it. I know it. Why else would I have been so heartsick when I heard he was promised to another? I did not and do not want to give him up to anyone." Her cheeks flushed. "Is it possible to fall in love so quickly?"

"It must be, if you have," Elizabeth replied. "I dare say that some love-matches are made in an instant while others can take years to develop. I do not think there is just one right way to fall in love."

"Good. I was worried for a moment that I was acting far too much like Lydia."

"The fact that you stopped to think about if you were acting too much like Lydia proves you were not." Elizabeth laughed, and Jane joined her until a cough overcame her.

"Are you sure you should be going down to breakfast?" As much as Elizabeth was eager to see her sister launch a campaign to secure her happy future, she just as equally had no desire to see Jane do so at the expense of her health.

"I am well enough to walk downstairs, eat, talk, and return to my bed. I will do no more than that."

Chapter 8

"MISS BENNET, MISS ELIZABETH," Mr. Bingley stood quickly to greet them as they entered the breakfast room. "We are delighted to have you join us this morning, are we not?" Though he asked the question of his companions, Mr. Darcy and Colonel Fitzwilliam, he spared not a look for either, but rather he kept his eyes on Jane and motioned to the chair next to him.

"We are indeed." Mr. Darcy's smile was as welcoming as any ever could be.

That particular gentleman's smile was an expression Elizabeth delighted to see. Since their talk in the garden four days ago, Mr. Darcy's smile seemed at the ready to be pulled out and put in place at a moment's notice, and there was an openness of character and presence about him that had not been there before. It was almost as if he were a whole new person.

Of course, she thought as she took a seat at the breakfast table next to the colonel, it was likely all due to his cousin's arrival on the same day. Whether that was the true reason or not, there was a large part of her who hoped it was because he wished for him and her to be friends.

"It has been a lonely two days," Colonel Fitzwilliam whispered once Elizabeth had taken a seat next to him. "Do agree to be in company more than twice today. Please?"

"Is your cousin so dull?" Elizabeth teased. For the past three days, since her conversation with Mr. Darcy and Colonel Fitzwilliam in the library during which she had agreed to stay, she had done her best to avoid Miss Bingley and Mrs. Hurst by only leaving Jane's side for some much-needed exercise or to fetch a new book to read. "For surely, you cannot mean that Mr. Bingley is dull."

Colonel Fitzwilliam chuckled. "We have wanted for agreeable female companionship."

"Were there no agreeable females in attendance at church yesterday?" Elizabeth's brow furrowed as she took a sip of the tea, which had just been placed in front of her by Mr. Darcy, while her eyes followed that very gentleman to the sideboard where Mr. Bingley was gathering a plate of food for Jane and, it seemed, Mr. Darcy was fetching a plate for her.

"My cousin can be a most obliging host himself. That is not a trait that only his friend possesses."

Elizabeth turned her attention to Colonel Fitzwilliam as her cheeks grew warm and likely brilliantly rosy. "About the ladies at church."

Again, the colonel chuckled. "If you would rather talk about that than my cousin, I will allow it."

"Why would I want to talk about your cousin?" Elizabeth kept her voice low so that said cousin would not hear her.

"You were watching him."

"I could have been watching Mr. Bingley."

"You could have been, but you were not." The colonel gave her a pointed and rather amused look to which she did not even flutter an eyelash in reply as she waited for him to answer her question about the ladies at church.

His lips twitched, and he turned his attention back to his plate of food. "I fear that I must report to you that the gathering of ladies at the church in Meryton is in short supply of agreeable ladies who are not pushing a daughter or themselves at available gentlemen."

Jane gasped as if surprised by the colonel's frankness.

"He is teasing," Elizabeth assured Jane. "You are teasing, are you not?" He had sounded as if he were.

"Mostly. There were several who made overtures of hopeful expectations." He rolled his eyes, and Jane smiled in understanding.

"I am certain one of those hopeful ladies was my mother," Jane said.

"She was, but you must know that I do not fault them. I am a fine catch." He winked at Jane who giggled softly before coughing.

Elizabeth had to agree that he would be a wonderful match for someone, perhaps even for a rather serious lady like her sister Mary.

"I find I know very little about you, Colonel, so I can neither agree nor disagree with your assessment of yourself," Jane said when she had recovered from her cough. "Elizabeth has told me all she knows about you because I have been curious, but she has spent nearly all her time trapped in my room, trying to entertain me."

"You need no entertainment." Elizabeth turned to look at the colonel just as Mr. Darcy placed a plate of food in front of her, so she thanked him before she continued. "Jane is the most long-suffering and agreeable patient any lady could ever hope to have under her care."

"I have been miserable with my wishing to go home." Jane gave Elizabeth an apologetic look before turning a smile on Mr. Bingley as he placed her food in front of her and then took a seat.

"Are you still determined to leave us as quickly as possible?" the colonel asked.

"My mother has said I must not. Therefore, I will remain until the day she thinks would be best for me to return home." Jane picked up her fork and knife. "And that means that I can now become acquainted with you, Mr.

Darcy, and Mr. Bingley." She speared a piece of ham and began cutting off a small piece.

"I am happy to hear it. What would you like to know?" the colonel asked. "But before you begin, you should know that I cannot reveal crown secrets or those told to me by your sister."

Elizabeth gasped, causing Colonel Fitzwilliam to laugh.

"He is a tease," Mr. Darcy said, inserting himself into the conversation. "That is likely the first thing you should know about my cousin. After that, you should know that he is as loyal to his friends as he is to his king. That is to say, his integrity is far less questionable than his sense of humour."

"I will have you know that my sense of humour is exceptional."

"I would not go that far in describing it," Mr. Bingley said. "Although I will admit to enjoying most of your teasing."

"Only the part that is not directed at you," Mr. Darcy added dryly.

Mr. Bingley shrugged one shoulder and smirked as if to say that Mr. Darcy was obviously correct.

Elizabeth watched the exchange with wonder. It was as if she had been let into the family quarters of a grand stately home only to find that the inhabitants of the house were very similar to her own family in how they interacted with each other.

"Do you have any siblings?" Jane asked the colonel. "Oh, wait, that is a foolish question. Of course, you have at least one brother. I blame my illness for not having thought of that before I spoke."

"It is a natural question." Colonel Fitzwilliam picked up his cup of tea. "I have one older brother and a younger one who is still in school. It seems he was something of an afterthought."

"What a dreadful thing to call your brother," Elizabeth cried as the colonel hid a smile behind the rim of his teacup before taking a drink.

"I did warn you that his sense of humour can be questionable," Mr. Darcy inserted.

"Indeed, you did," Elizabeth agreed.

"There would be four of them if every child had survived," Mr. Darcy added.

"Oh! That is very sad." Jane looked at Colonel Fitzwilliam with eyes that brimmed with watery sympathy.

The colonel shook his head as he returned his cup to the table. "I was too young to remember much about the ordeal. He or she would have been born the year after Darcy was, which means I was little more than a year old when Mother lost the baby. Therefore, the only grief I feel over the loss is for my mother and father, and even that feels distant."

"It is still sad," Jane asserted.

"I would not argue against that fact," the colonel assured her. "A loss of an innocent life should be grieved. But returning to my younger brother, Robert. I have always teased him about being an afterthought because there is a rather large gap of time – eight years – between us. Of course, he has always teased me in return that it was because I was such a tribulation to our parents that they could not even tolerate the thought of another child, let alone produce one, until they realized they might need him since there was every reason to believe I might die and leave them without a spare to the title, given my tendency to favour rambunctious pursuits from an early age."

"Indeed?" Jane said. "Well, that is quite the argument."

"It is a well-founded one. He is currently studying law. It is a profession which I think suits him quite well."

"Do you love your older brother as much as your younger one?" Jane asked.

"I did not say I loved Robert."

"Not in so many words, but I heard it."

"As did I," Elizabeth agreed.

"Take care, ladies," Mr. Bingley inserted, "we would not wish for the colonel's devil-may-care, take-no-prisoners reputation to be tarnished with sentimental truths."

The colonel shook his head and chuckled. "I think I can tolerate the world knowing that I adore my youngest brother and suffer my older one quite well."

"Well enough to be the namesake of the viscount's first born," Mr. Darcy added.

"That is lovely!" Jane cried. "I have always assumed there might be jealousy between brothers who have been born and not born to a title. I suppose that assumption is based on all the history of England that Father insisted we must know."

"My father did once make me swear an oath that I would not lob off my brother's head or leave him locked in the dungeon –"

"Wine cellar," Mr. Darcy corrected.

"Very well, it was a wine cellar and not a dungeon in truth, but we were playing knights and dragons."

Elizabeth laughed. "We played knights and dragons when we were young as well."

"Who was the damsel who needed rescuing?" Mr. Bingley asked.

"Oh, that was always Jane," Elizabeth replied.

"That was usually an unfortunate dog or cat for us," Richard said.

"Were you the knight or the dragon?" Jane asked the colonel.

"I was usually the dragon since the viscount held a title and therefore, rightly deserved to be the knight, or so he said."

Elizabeth chuckled as she imagined the colonel and his brother arguing over who was allowed to play which role in the game.

"Lizzy was always our dragon," Jane continued, "which left Mary to attempt to rescue me despite her less than helpful fellow knights, who were too easily distracted by ribbons and kittens."

"Which the dragon used to her advantage." Oh, how Mary would lecture, first, Kitty and then, Lydia, when she was old enough to join the game, about keeping their eyes on the task at hand. It had done little good.

"Mary finally decided it was best if her two easily distracted knights were left at the palace to make sure the princess had a pretty room to come home to," Jane said. "And that is when Lizzy began to find it much harder to defeat the knight."

"Mary can be a formidable opponent when her mind is set on something," Elizabeth added with a glance towards the colonel. She should maybe tell Jane about her suspicions regarding Mary's admiration for Mr. Darcy's cousin.

"Mary is nearly as stubborn as Lizzy." Jane smiled sweetly.

"I say she is more stubborn."

Jane merely shrugged and smiled, which was how Jane often disagreed with Elizabeth. It was much harder to argue with a shrug than it was with words, and Jane knew it.

"I understand you have a sister, Mr. Darcy." Jane's eyes held Elizabeth's for a moment as she asked the question.

"I do." He looked towards Elizabeth.

"It was actually Miss Bingley who told me about her," Jane clarified.

"Miss Bingley told you about Georgiana?" Mr. Darcy's question was suffused with surprise.

"That is a lovely name, and from how wonderful I have been told she is, I am sure it is very fitting." Jane paused and turned to Mr. Bingley. "Is Miss Darcy all that is lovely?"

He seemed shocked to be asked such a question. "I suppose she is." He looked at his friends, who both nodded.

"I figured you would say she is. One does not pledge himself to a lady if he does not think of her as the loveliest woman in the world, now, does he?" Jane was wearing a very convincing look of innocence as she let her gaze wander from gentleman to gentleman.

Elizabeth pressed her lips together and attempted to look neither amused by nor proud of her sister's ability to press her cause so well.

"Pledge?" The colonel was the first of their stunned companions to recover his ability to speak. "Georgiana is not pledged to anyone. There is not something Darcy and

I need to know, is there?" He leveled a formidable glare at Mr. Bingley, who sputtered a *no*.

Jane's expression faltered for a moment before settling into one of feigned confusion. "But your sisters said they were anxious for the day when your family and Mr. Darcy's would be joined and that they were delighted to be gaining a sister like Miss Darcy. I know I did not hear them incorrectly even if my head was aching at the time."

"Did my sisters say I was going to marry Miss Darcy?" Mr. Bingley looked horrified.

"Perhaps not in those words, but they were very clear that they were happy you had found such a good match."

"Are you certain they were not hinting at Caroline marrying Darcy?" Mr. Bingley asked.

Elizabeth pulled in a quick breath and looked first at Colonel Fitzwilliam, who had told her it was not an option when she had posed the question a few days ago, and then, at Mr. Darcy, who was scowling.

"No," Jane answered as if she was unsure if she should give an answer or not. "Is that a possibility?"

"It most certainly is not." Mr. Darcy answered before Mr. Bingley could. "Miss Bingley might want it to be, but it is not." He shook his head. "Nor is it a possibility that my sister is promised to Bingley – not that I would not approve of him for her if that was how things were and she was old enough to be presented with an offer." His expression softened. "Georgiana is not yet out. There is still one season before I have to face that ordeal."

"She will do well." Elizabeth did not know why she felt compelled to comfort him, but she did. Perhaps it was because she knew how much he cared for his sister. That fact had been obvious from their conversation in the library.

Mr. Darcy gave her a small, grateful smile. "Thank you. I believe she will do well. What I am uncertain about is if I will."

"We will weather it together," Colonel Fitzwilliam assured him. "And if you do as your father says, you may have a wife to help you through it as well."

Elizabeth's eyes grew wide. "Will we soon be wishing you happy?" Strangely, that idea seemed to sit rather ill with her.

Mr. Darcy sighed. "My father's final letter is advice for finding a wife and a plea to not put it off."

How interesting. She would dearly love to hear the advice that had been given, but it would be far too forward to ask about that.

"Please, do not mention it to Miss Bingley," Mr. Darcy whispered before rising, along with the colonel, as Miss Bingley and Mrs. Hurst entered the breakfast room.

"You will have to eat in your rooms." Mr. Bingley had not moved from his place of repose and motioned for Mr.

Darcy and the colonel to be seated. "There is no room for you here."

"Do not be silly, Charles," Mrs. Hurst said. "There are yet four chairs at the table and another two can be squeezed in if needed."

"The chairs may be empty, but I assure you they are not available. Miss Bennet needs quiet to properly recover, and I am unwilling to allow you and Caroline to keep her from it."

"I will be finished soon."

Elizabeth gave her sister a look that she hoped Jane read as 'stop being so obliging' because that is what it was supposed to mean.

"Do not hurry on account of my sisters. This is my home, and I say you may remain as you are for as long as you like. Indeed, I am certain you could remain here for always and I would not be opposed to it." He folded his arms across his chest.

"Really, Charles, do be reasonable. Miss Bennet will be needed at home eventually," Miss Bingley said. "And Louisa and I will whisper."

Mr. Bingley shook his head. "Gather your food and be gone. I have no desire for your presence while I finish my meal."

"You cannot mean it," Mrs. Hurst said.

"I am quite certain I do. Hurst, you may stay if you wish."

Mr. Hurst looked torn for a moment as he glanced between the table and his wife.

"Miss Bennet has just congratulated me on my upcoming marriage. Did you know I was betrothed, Hurst?"

The man shook his head and glanced at his wife. "Should I have known that?"

"I do not see how you should be required to know something that I did not even know," Mr. Bingley answered.

"Do I wish to ask to whom you are betrothed?" Mr. Hurst took a seat at the table cautiously, clearly distancing himself from his wife and sister-in-law.

"Apparently, he is betrothed to my sister," Mr. Darcy said without a hint of amusement. "Yet, he has never courted her, she is not out, and I have not been consulted. I dare say that is grounds for a parting of ways between myself and Bingley."

"Oh, is that all. Miss Bennet must have misunderstood," Mrs. Hurst said quickly. "It was merely a hope that was shared with her and not a fact." She gave Jane a condescending look. "After all, dear Jane was not feeling well. Ladies should not ride in the rain."

Elizabeth watched as Jane squared her shoulders. It was a sure sign that there was fiery indignation burning behind Jane's sweet façade.

"Ladies should not lie to other ladies about their brother and his particular friend's sister. At least, they should not if they value the friendship between their brother and his friend. I know what was said. There was no misunderstanding aside from the one where I considered you to be my friend." She stood. "Elizabeth, I have eaten enough and am feeling fatigued. Would you accompany me to my room?"

"Gladly."

It was perhaps the most dramatic exit Jane had ever made and even Elizabeth's desire to finish her breakfast would not keep her from being at her sister's side as she made her grand departure.

"I can have something sent up if you want it," the colonel offered.

"Perhaps tea in about an hour?" Elizabeth whispered in reply. "Maybe with a biscuit or two?"

The colonel nodded his agreement, and Elizabeth joined Jane in leaving the room. However, Jane did not leave directly. Apparently, her most dramatic exit was about to rise to higher heights, for instead of heading straight for the door, Jane stopped just in front of Miss Bingley and Mrs. Hurst.

"Just so there are no further misunderstandings, you should know that I am not leaving until tomorrow as prescribed by my mother," she said quietly, but not so softly that no one at the table would hear her. "Nor am

I giving up your brother as I know your conversation at dinner was designed to make me do." Then, she turned, smiled at that very gentleman, and wished him a good morning.

Chapter 9

Darcy tapped lightly on the door to Miss Bennet's chamber and then, shifted from foot to foot as he waited for someone to answer. It was not at all the thing to do for a gentleman to call on a lady in her bed chamber, but circumstances were such that it was necessary. Propriety would just have to be understanding of that. He lifted his hand to tap once again just as the door opened.

"Mr. Darcy?"

"I apologize for coming here."

Aside from her surprised expression, Miss Elizabeth had a relaxed air about her that heightened the intimacy of their current location and deepened the feeling of impropriety. Darcy darted a look down the hall to see if anyone had seen him.

"Would it be possible for you to join me for a walk? Perhaps Miss Bennet could join us in the garden? Mr. Bingley and my cousin will accompany us, of course." The words tumbled awkwardly from his mouth. He had tried to get one of them to come with him to make this request, but they both thought that it would draw far too much attention for more than one of them to take on this task. However, either one of them would have presented the offer more smoothly than he was currently doing.

"Is something wrong?"

Should he indicate that there was, indeed, something amiss, or should he leave that to be discovered? Deciding to err on the side of openness, Darcy gave one nod. He would want to know the truth if he were the one asking the question.

"Perhaps," he added. It was not as if anything untoward had happened to Miss Elizabeth's sisters – yet – but Miss Mary had certainly thought something might.

Miss Elizabeth's brow furrowed. "You do not know?"

"Not completely, but I understand from what I have been told that the trouble is of an urgent nature," he explained. Miss Mary had most certainly looked distressed enough for him to believe the matter required immediate consideration by her elder sisters.

Miss Elizabeth turned away from him and back towards the interior of the room. "Jane, do you feel well enough to sit in the garden with Mr. Bingley?"

"Oh, yes!" came the cry from within. "I would dearly love to do something other than sit in here."

"That settles it. We will join you shortly," Miss Elizabeth said to Darcy before adding. "Should I be worried?"

Darcy's shoulders raised and lowered. "I am not entirely certain about that either." But he would be worried. "I do not wish to speak of it here, but we met your sister while we were out for an afternoon ride." It would be more accurate to say they were trying to avoid Bingley's sisters, both of whom currently possessed rather foul tempers.

"Which sister?"

"Miss Mary," he replied while mentally scolding himself for not having specified that information. Truly, Richard or Bingley would have done a much better job of this.

"She looked rather out of sorts when we saw her," he continued, "and after some persuasion by Bingley and my cousin, she agreed to let us carry her message to you rather than returning home and finding a stable boy or footman to bring it to you."

His hands were sweating inside his gloves and prickly bits of energy were racing up his spine. The longer he stood here, the greater chance there was of his being seen at the door of a lady's bedchamber. "I really must go."

"Of course. We will be quick."

He accepted her remarks and expressed his thanks with a nod of his head before turning to hurry away.

"Mr. Darcy," she called after him when he had only managed three steps toward the stairs.

"Yes, Miss Elizabeth?"

"Is she well?"

He smiled at her concern. It was exactly what he would ask about his sister as well. "Yes, no one is ill or in grave danger." He saw her visibly relax in front of him.

"We will be down directly."

This time, he waited until she had closed the door before he continued on his way toward the garden.

"Mr. Darcy, you simply must come sit with us," Mrs. Hurst joined him as he descended the stairs.

"I cannot." Even if he did not need to be in the garden when Miss Elizabeth got there, he would not be interested in sitting with Louisa and Caroline.

"Oh, but you truly must. Caroline and I are so very bored. Surely, you cannot still be angry with us over a small misunderstanding."

Darcy's jaw clenched. It had been no misunderstanding, and the tale that had been told was no trifling matter.

"I believe Miss Bennet had the purpose of your dinner conversation correct when she spoke to you before she left the breakfast room this morning. I do not believe for a moment that it was a misunderstanding on her part, nor can I imagine what you were thinking when you used my sister in your scheme." He pressed his lips together, drew a breath through his nose, and slowly released it before continuing. "I think it is best if you and your sister do not seek me out for some time. I value your brother's friendship and have made him a promise to help him settle into Netherfield. It would grieve me most profoundly to have to break my word to him just so I could avoid his sisters."

His words seemed to have little effect on Louisa as she did not even let him get a step ahead of her, and he was taking the steps quickly in a failing effort to put distance between him and her.

"I do not know why you would be upset about our wish to have Georgiana eventually – after she has had her come out, of course – matched with our brother. She is everything that is sweet and agreeable, and I do think they would get on quite well." She scampered to keep up with him as he increased his pace further. "And it would be an advantageous pairing. She could lend Charles the status he deserves, while he could ease her way into social situations, since she tends to be reserved."

"Is this what both you and your sister think?" Darcy came to a stop at the bottom of the stairs. Was his sister only important to them for her position in society? And was their brother's whole worth as a husband only to be found in his amiable nature?

"It is indeed. Neither of us are lacking in our understanding of what makes a good marriage."

They were if they only thought that rank and being a charming dinner guest were the deciding factors of who should marry whom. "I think you are."

Mrs. Hurst's eyes grew wide as she gasped. Apparently, she had not expected him to disagree with her.

"I assure you, Mr. Darcy, that mine and Caroline's training has been exceptional on all fronts."

He shook his head. "I fear there is at least one thing you have overlooked entirely, and to my way of thinking, it is the most important item of all."

"I do not think I have." Her tone was one of utter disbelief with a touch of ridicule. He had heard her use that tone to disparage many people in the time he had known her. Of course, he had never expected to be one of those unfortunates.

He turned toward the door. The quicker he could be away from her, the better.

"Then, you are also mistaken about that," he said, "for you have entirely neglected the element of the heart in making a match. I know that not all will agree with me on this, but they do not need to. I will not allow my sister's heart to be forgotten when it comes to helping her select a husband."

His father had made it plain that both of his children were to remember their hearts when choosing their future mates, and Darcy would not fail him in this. That part of his father's most recent letter had been sitting heavily on his mind since he read it.

The reason for his careful contemplation of that instruction could be heard above him in the hallway with her sister. He gave Mrs. Hurst a bow and moved toward the door, which was now being held open for him. Bingley's butler was good at reading when a gentleman needed a quick escape.

"Charles is easy to love," Mrs. Hurst followed him to the door as she pressed her point.

"I will not disagree with you, but I will point out that he has found his heart leading him to a lady who is not my sister."

"But he could do so much better. It is an infatuation, nothing more. If we were to leave Netherfield after this ball he has promised to host, I am certain he would forget about her and find another to hold his interest until Georgiana is of age."

Had she not heard a word he had said? He caught a flutter of movement on the stairs from the corner of his eye.

"You, yourself, have said that the Bennets are lacking," Louisa continued.

Darcy's heart raced. Were Miss Elizabeth and her sister close enough to hear that? "I should not have."

Louisa's head pulled back in shock.

"They are a family with quirks and oddities just as any other family."

"Do you now condone the behaviour of the youngest Bennets and their mother?"

That was a tricky question to answer honestly since he was not sure he did approve of their behaviour. That being said, it was not as if he truly knew them intimately. He smiled. That was where the answer was found, was it not? He was certain his father would say it was.

"I cannot honestly say without becoming better acquainted." Which is what he should have done from the beginning. That thought did not settle gently into his mind. In fact, that error rather poked and twisted, causing him to feel very uncomfortable with how he had been since his arrival and up until that morning in the garden with Miss Elizabeth.

"You cannot truly mean that you are planning to make the Bennets your friends?" Louisa's voice was high and loud.

That would have been heard by Miss Elizabeth and her sister even if they were not halfway down the stairs as they currently were.

Darcy clenched his jaw and fixed a steely glare on Louisa. "Let me make myself plain, madame. I have not been what I should have been. I have said things and behaved in ways that did me no credit and have tarnished my family's name in the neighbourhood. I have seen the error of my ways as presented to me by my father in the letters he left to me. I will not willingly and ignorantly continue in the same vein. Therefore, you must believe me when I say that I intend to not only make the Bennets my friends, but I also intend to extend myself in making acquaintances of others in the neighbourhood." Even if that was likely to tax his abilities to a staggering degree.

He motioned for the butler to keep the door open by lifting one finger. Then, he turned to the stairs. "Ladies," he said with a smile, "would you care to join me in the garden?"

Miss Elizabeth looked at Mrs. Hurst and then back at Darcy. "It would be our pleasure, would it not, Jane?"

"It most certainly would." Miss Bennet smiled one of her serene smiles and did not even cast a look in Louisa's direction as she and her sister came to where he was. "Have you been out? Is it warm?"

"Quite," he assured her. Not that she had any reason to fear becoming chilled, as either she or her sister had seen to it that she was well ensconced in wraps. "You will inform me if you wish to return to the house?"

"She will," Miss Elizabeth said as she slipped her arm around one of his proffered arms and Miss Bennet took the other.

"My, my," Louisa said with a sneer, "are you not just all charmingly arranged?"

Darcy looked to his left and then his right. "I do think you finally got something right, Mrs. Hurst." And with that, he finally left the house.

Chapter 10

Elizabeth plopped down, very unceremoniously, next to Jane on the garden bench and read Mary's hasty note again.

"What is it? What is the trouble?" Jane leaned towards her and began reading over Elizabeth's shoulder.

"Soldiers and a parson," Elizabeth muttered as she passed the letter to Jane. "My two youngest sisters are quite infatuated with anyone in a red coat." She smiled at the colonel. "It was a good thing that you were not wearing one the day you met them."

He chuckled. "A red coat does draw attention from many a lady. I will own that I do not mind it so very much, unless my mother is near."

"I do hope that the ladies who fall at your feet are older than Lydia and Kitty." Elizabeth's youngest sisters were incurable flirts at present. She expected they would mature their way out of it eventually, but of course, by then, it might be too late to correct the damage such behaviour was capable of causing.

The colonel shook his head. "Not always. But do not worry; I turn them away as gently as I can. Now, what is it about these soldiers that is a problem – other than your sister's young age."

"It seems," Jane said, "that Lydia and Kitty have been called on by two officers, and today, these two officers mentioned a new friend who was arriving from town and joining himself to the militia. He arrives tomorrow, and Lydia has persuaded Mama that it is *absolutely necessary* to go to town for ribbons and lace as soon as may be." She glanced at Mr. Bingley. "They are needed to prepare for a particular ball to which they just received an invitation."

"Ah, yes, I dashed it off this morning," Mr. Bingley said with a smile. "I did not trust my sisters to actually send invitations to all whom I wished to have come to my ball, so I have several invitations that have either been sent or are in the process of being made ready. Sir William also received his today. I thought it best if he were among the first to be invited."

"That is an excellent idea," Jane agreed. "Sir William does pride himself on being in the know and on all the lists for soirees."

"I thought he might be so," Mr. Bingley said. "I am sorry I did not wait if the receipt of my invitation is creating troubles for you, however."

"No, no," Jane assured him.

Elizabeth watched the way her sister and Mr. Bingley so naturally fell into conversation with one another and bowed to the other or lent assurance as needed. They would do very well together, and that meant she had one less sister about whom she needed to worry.

"Lydia and Kitty would find another excuse to go to town to meet a new gentleman rather than waiting for Papa to meet him and then, introduce them." Jane sighed and shook her head.

"Do your sisters think your father would not approve of this fellow?" Mr. Darcy asked.

"They think that it would be too long to wait to find out," Elizabeth answered. Lydia's store of patience was appallingly low. "Papa is not always quick to greet all the newcomers to the area, or even when he is, he often makes my youngest sisters wait and pester him for a time before he tells them what he knows. I do not know why he does it, but he does." It was not as if it gained him any of his dearly loved peace, nor did it seem to teach her sisters patience at all.

"I think he does it because he likes how Mama gets so excited to hear that he has done what she thought he had not," Jane said.

"Do you?" Elizabeth asked.

"Oh, yes! Have you never watched his face when Mama and our sisters are effusing about his slyness?"

"I must admit that I have not." Most often, Elizabeth had been occupied with watching her sisters and mother. It had never occurred to her to observe her father.

"You should. It is one of the times when you can see how much he adores Mama."

Elizabeth shook her head in bewilderment. "And yet, he torments and teases her." A little too much if you asked her.

"I know it is quite the paradox, but I just think it is how they are."

Elizabeth would have to pay better attention to that when she got home. She had always thought that she did not want a marriage like her parent's, but perhaps, she had gotten that wrong. Perhaps they were happier than she had accounted for.

"Then, I take it that Miss Mary is worried about the impropriety of them meeting with these officers without your father?" Colonel Fitzwilliam asked, neatly directing the conversation back to where it began.

"No," Jane replied, "they are not doing it secretly. They have been granted permission to go to town and if they happen upon their officers, it is perfectly agreeable to our father that they be introduced since Mary will be with them, and they will also have the company of our father's cousin when they go."

"Your father's cousin? I did not know he had a cousin." Mr. Bingley took the letter from Jane when she offered it to him to read.

"Mr. Collins is a distant cousin whose father has been estranged from my father for years. It seems that this Mr. Collins has arrived –"

"To find a wife among his cousins?" Mr. Bingley cried.

"Yes," Elizabeth answered. "That is why it is even more important to Lydia and Kitty to go to town to secure their officers if they can so they can avoid Mr. Collins."

"Miss Mary certainly does not paint him in a favourable light," Mr. Bingley said. "Oh, dear," he added. "Your mother thinks Miss Mary would make an exceptional parson's wife?"

Elizabeth nodded. "Mary is serious."

She was certain that their mother only understood Lydia when it came to her daughters. She seemed to see them how they presented themselves rather than looking deeper to the private moments when their true natures blossomed. It was not unkindly done. It was as Jane would say, *just how she was*. She was no great intellect, but she was their mother and so, they loved her despite her shortcomings.

"Miss Mary? A parson's wife?" Colonel Fitzwilliam moved to stand behind Bingley and read the letter from there.

"That is not the worst of it." Mr. Bingley, whose expression had darkened, held the letter so that the colonel could read it more easily and pointed to something further down the page.

A rumble of something truly terrifying came from the colonel.

"We will meet them in Meryton," he said decisively. "What time do you think they will be there?" He looked from Jane to Elizabeth.

"Why?" Mr. Darcy asked cautiously as he took the letter from Bingley.

The colonel did not reply but rather, crossed his arms and watched as Darcy read.

"No," Mr. Darcy whispered.

"Ah, you found the reason," the colonel said.

Panic rose within Elizabeth, and she struggled to tamp it down. "I still do not know what the issue is, and I would like to know, since it seems whatever it is poses more danger to my sisters than I have already imagined."

Mr. Darcy drew and released a breath. "Do you remember what I told you about my sister when we were in the library? About how her heart was broken?"

Jane gasped and looked at Elizabeth.

"I do," Elizabeth replied. "But Jane does not know about that."

Mr. Darcy favoured her with a small smile. Was it his thanks for keeping what she knew of his sister's distress to herself?

He turned a similarly soft expression to Jane. "This fellow, Mr. Wickham, whom your sisters are supposed to meet, is the person who pretended to love my sister this past summer only to leave her with a broken heart." Mr. Darcy looked at his cousin. "Mr. Wickham had convinced Georgiana to elope with him."

Elizabeth drew in a quick and deep breath of air and clutched Jane's hand. Her youngest sisters were no match for such a practiced charlatan.

"I arrived unexpectedly at Ramsgate where my sister was staying with her companion and put an end to their plans when I told Wickham that he would not receive any of Georgiana's money, which is substantial."

"He only loved her money," Jane whispered.

Lydia and Kitty had no money, so perhaps they were not in as much danger as the colonel and Mr. Darcy thought.

"Exactly so," Mr. Darcy returned the paper he held to Jane. "Mr. Wickham is not pleased with me for that and other reasons. You see, we grew up together. He was the son of my father's steward as well as my father's godson. He was left an inheritance which he has been given, but that he thinks should be given to him again."

"How?" Elizabeth pressed her lips together. It was not her place to ask about all the particulars.

"It is a natural question," Mr. Darcy assured her with that same small smile from before. It was a very charming expression. If he used it more often, he would have ladies falling over themselves to be at his side for more than his ten thousand a year and his grand estate.

"My father left Mr. Wickham a living that was under his power to bestow. At the time when my father died, Mr. Wickham was set on studying law and not taking orders, which was for the best. He is not of the proper disposition to take orders." Mr. Darcy shared a meaningful look with his cousin.

"To put it mildly," the colonel muttered.

Ah, that was likely the danger to her sisters. This Mr. Wickham must be something of a rake.

"Therefore," Mr. Darcy continued, "he accepted a sum of money in place of the living, but after squandering it and the living falling open, he came back to me, expecting to be given it. I denied him, of course. So, that, along with having kept him from gaining Georgie's money, has left a gulf of hard feelings between us."

"Were you friends when you were young?" Jane asked.

Mr. Darcy's expression turned sad as he nodded. "We were never overly close, but we were friends."

Elizabeth's heart ached for the pain the man before her had experienced at the hands of a friend, and if Mr. Wickham would treat his friends so shabbily, then who knew what he would do to two naïve young ladies whom he had no reason to care for. The colonel was correct. They must intercept her sisters and see to their safety.

"I would expect my sisters to walk out after breakfast," she said. "Perhaps by half ten?"

"Then, we will go riding at half ten," the colonel said.

"No, *we* will take the carriage," Jane countered with a rarely seen expression that brooked no objections. Of course, it swiftly faded as she turned to Mr. Bingley. "That is if it is agreeable to you."

"Whatever you wish is yours," he replied.

Oh, yes, Elizabeth believed that wholeheartedly. Everything that was Mr. Bingley's would soon also be Mrs. Bingley's.

"We will not all fit comfortably. I will ride ahead," the colonel inserted.

"And I will write to my mother and tell her of Mr. Bingley's generous offer to take Elizabeth and me to town before he brings us home so that we can get what we need to prepare for his ball, and we will meet our sisters there so that we can coordinate our purchases," Jane said.

"That is very well-thought-out," the colonel commended. "Miss Bennet is not just a pretty face, Bingley. I'd not let her go if I were you."

Mr. Bingley grinned. "I have no intentions of letting her go. In fact," he said as he stared off into the distance. "Perhaps..." He paused for a moment before continuing. "Perhaps I could speak to your father tomorrow to let him know of my intentions to see if we will suit?" He turned toward Jane. "Then, I will not have to worry about your cousin even attempting to woo you."

Jane ducked her head as she smiled, but then, instead of demurely granting Mr. Bingley her permission to speak to her father, she lifted her head and drew her shoulders back. Elizabeth could not help but smile at seeing her sister so determined and being so in company. Jane was rarely forward about anything. However, when she was set on gaining something of importance, she had been known to stand her ground with vigour.

"You have no reason to fear." Her cheeks grew rosy. "I cannot be wooed by anyone but you."

"Then, I have your permission to speak to your father?"

Could a gentleman look more delighted than Mr. Bingley did at this moment? Elizabeth was certain it was not possible.

"Yes, of course."

Elizabeth turned her eyes from her sister to Mr. Darcy to see what his reaction was.

Meeting her eyes, he extended his hand to her and tipped his head toward the path to their right.

Happily, she placed her hand in his and rose to leave her sister with Mr. Bingley. Jane would be well-cared-for – not just now, but for always – and Elizabeth could now turn her attention to her next youngest sister's heart's desire and the task of keeping Lydia and Kitty from being charmed by a scoundrel and his friends.

Chapter 11

DARCY PACED THE LENGTH of the library and back again. It was a pity the room was not more sizeable.

"Let us consider this logically." Richard sat near a table with a light on it as he read Darcy's father's letter. "How long have you known her now?"

"Since I arrived in Hertfordshire, or nearly so."

"And that was at the end of September, and we are more than halfway through November, which makes it not yet two months."

Darcy shook his head. "Yes, I know how long I have been at Netherfield."

"Have you truly had enough time to evaluate Miss Elizabeth?"

Darcy stopped midway between his cousin and the far end of the library. "Are you saying it would be foolish to make my affections known to her?"

He had not expected that from his cousin. Normally, his cousin was only second to Bingley in picking up a scheme to see Darcy consider a possible wife. That is not to say that it had happened often – maybe three times in the past five years – but whenever Darcy began to wonder if a particular lady was worth pursuing, Richard would be there in person or letter, urging him to discover if his heart and future would be happy with whomever it was. Not once had his cousin ever cautioned him to take his time until now.

"No, not at all. I think she is a fabulously charming young woman. I just do not wish for you to regret later that you did not do your due diligence in contemplation."

"Are you saying then that nearly two months is not long enough?"

Richard looked up from the letter. "Have you been considering her since you arrived?"

Darcy scrubbed a hand down his face. "I did not know I was, but yes, I do believe I have been. She ties my thoughts in knots, Richard. Please, just help me untangle the knots without adding any new ones. Unless, of course, they are necessary to save me from an unhappy fate."

The key turned in the lock and all conversation in the library stopped until the door opened to admit Bingley.

"Has Miss Bennet gone to bed?" Darcy asked.

"She has." He locked the door behind him. "Caroline and Louisa are rather put out with us for refusing to be in any room where they are." He chuckled as he removed his coat and tossed it on a sofa near where Richard was sitting.

Bingley had barred his sisters from the dining room, insisting that they take their meal elsewhere, and, then after dinner, he had refused them admittance to the drawing room where he was spending the evening near a fire with Miss Bennet and Miss Elizabeth. Richard and Darcy had retired here to the library ahead of Bingley and before the Bennet ladies had gone above stairs. Their early departure from the drawing room had been completely Darcy's doing.

Ever since Darcy had heard that Mr. Collins was at Longbourn looking for a wife, he had been as eager as Bingley to declare himself to the lady who filled his thoughts from first thing in the morning to last thing at night before taking up delightful residence in his dreams.

"What has Darcy wearing a rut into the floor in here?" Bingley lounged on the couch with his legs extended out in front of him and his arms resting along the back of the piece of furniture.

"May I?" Richard held the letter up to indicate to Darcy what he was asking permission to do.

"Yes." Darcy turned away from them and began pacing again. One foot in front of the other, creating a soothing rhythmic pace.

He knew every word that was in that letter, and those words swirled in his mind as he walked.

Do not wait, Fitzwilliam. Find someone to be your companion, not just your wife. You and she must be happy together despite the arrival or non-arrival of children. She must be someone you can look to in joy to multiply your delight and in sorrow for comfort. She must be someone who holds the power to fill your heart to overflowing with happiness with her presence or crush it with grief at her departure.

In short, I want you to have what I had for the brief time your mother was mine. Do not wait. Find her now. I know you will put it off until Georgiana is grown. It is how you are, but to do so would be a mistake. It will make it harder to help your sister find what she deserves if you have never known it yourself.

Choose someone who is intelligent and charming. Choose someone who will tend to Pemberley as it deserves, but do not put that above your heart. First and foremost, make sure your wife can tend to your heart and those of your children.

You have no need of money. Do not choose a wife purely for her wealth or station. If she meets all the requirements above: charming, intelligent, capable of managing a large estate, and she loves you as you love her, then, you have found the only lady I would ever agree to let you marry.

Three months.

That is your goal for finding her if you wish for my desire to give you the greatest gift of all on your twenty-eighth birthday. You have never not taken up a challenge that I have put before you. I pray that this will not be the time you choose to change your ways.

(And as I write those words, I hear your mother whisper in my ear, as she did many times in her life, 'Trust him, my dear, he will be as good a man as ever was, for he has you to guide him.' I am not sure she was completely correct on that. I have made my errors, but I do hope I have passed on enough good to see you happily into your future.)

Bingley let out a long slow whistle. "This is a weighty letter."

That it was.

"Three months is not very long to find a future Mrs. Darcy," Bingley added.

"It is plenty of time if he has already met her," Richard inserted.

When Darcy turned towards them, Bingley was grinning broadly just as Darcy had suspected from the tone of voice his friend had used when speaking about finding a Mrs. Darcy.

"I told you two months ago what I thought of Miss Elizabeth and you," Bingley said.

"I have not forgotten, but we had only just met. How was I to know that you were correct about how well she suited me? It was not as if our first meeting was the sort that recommends one to another."

"That is because it was not a meeting at all for you," Bingley said. "However, I had spent a bit of time with her, and her sister had spoken so highly of her that I knew enough to suspect." He chuckled. "And then, when she refused to dance with you at Sir William's? Hah! Then. Then, I truly knew she was the perfect lady for you. Your father does not say it here, but anyone who knows you for longer than a fortnight knows you need someone who will not bend to your every demand – well, that is, anyone who is brighter than my sisters knows it."

Richard barked in laughter. "He has you there, Darcy. You need a lady who will stand toe-to-toe with you when needed. I could see Miss Elizabeth doing that."

"And you know she is not after your money or your estate," Bingley added. "Ladies who are looking to marry you for the prize of wealth do not avoid you or argue with you." He waved a hand toward the door. "Look at my sister if you need proof that what I say is true." He sighed audibly. "But most importantly and most seriously, Miss Elizabeth will make you a better Darcy."

"She already has," Darcy said. Sure, it was his father's letter that had pointed out his poor behaviour to him, but it was Miss Elizabeth's opinion of him which had made him feel the weight of shame his ill manners deserved.

"Then, let us look at this logically," Richard repeated. "What do you know about her?"

"She will love your sister and your children," Bingley offered, holding up a finger to mark his first point. "She has cared very well for Miss Bennet." He put up a second finger. "She will comport herself with dignity, for she bears her mother and sisters' behaviour with grace and has yet to speak to either of my sisters in the way in which they deserve to be spoken to." He put up a third finger. "She is both intelligent and charming. I should hope I do not need to give you an example to support that claim." He put up a fourth finger. "And I think she could be fairly easily persuaded to like you, for it does seem she is more willing to be in your presence now than she was when she first arrived at Netherfield."

"She watches him," Richard said.

"Does she?" Darcy had never noticed Miss Elizabeth watching him.

"She is cautious, but I am trained to be observant. Bingley is right. I do think you stand a chance. Present yourself to her. I think your father would approve."

"You are absolutely convinced that it is not too soon?"

"I have nearly proposed in the time it has taken you to decide you might like a lady." Bingley scoffed. "I most certainly am not going to tell you it is too soon. And you must remember that there is that cousin of theirs." He gave Darcy a meaningful look. "If you are not going to declare yourself to Miss Elizabeth, you should at least let Mrs. Bennet know you might be interested in her daughter. I would wager my inheritance and my sister's dowry and be stuck with her forever on the fact that your ten thousand pounds would be enough for Mrs. Bennet to dissuade

Mr. Collins if he decided upon Miss Elizabeth over Miss Mary."

That was likely true. "She did seem eager to present Miss Elizabeth to me for consideration when she was here that morning."

"Eager as a hound who has smelled the fox and wishes to give chase," Richard agreed with a laugh. "I dare say you are the reason she has decided that Miss Mary would make a good parson's wife." He shook his head. "I do not see it."

"I do," Bingley inserted. "I did not say so before since Miss Elizabeth did not seem to think it was a good idea, but I do see how Miss Mary, with her austere nature, could be a good parson's wife."

"She is too young," Richard protested.

"There are ladies who are married by the time they reach Miss Mary's age," Bingley countered.

Richard scowled. "Miss Mary does not seem to think she is destined to be a parson's wife."

"Perhaps she is too young to know that," Bingley said with a smirk.

"I doubt that," Richard replied. "And you are not as clever as you think you are."

"Oh, I think I am."

Darcy shook his head. This was not an unfamiliar scene upon which he was looking. Richard and Bingley often had friendly squabbles over differing opinions. It was better to end it now rather than letting it deteriorate to the point where one or the other called on him to take up their side, for both had good points.

"Bingley is clever. Miss Mary is young but not too young, and if she does not want to consider marrying Mr. Collins, she should not be forced to do so."

"You truly do not know how to have a good time, do you?" Bingley teased.

"I know I do not want to hear you both carrying on when I am attempting to make a decision of some significance."

"Marry her," Bingley said on the end of a yawn. "Then, we will be brothers." He stifled another yawn.

"Tired, old man?" Richard taunted.

Perhaps Darcy should have let these two argue about Miss Mary, for it appeared things were going to devolve into some sort of debate anyway.

"Tired, but not old," Bingley retorted. "I leave that role to you and Darcy."

"I am not old," Darcy protested before he could think better of being drawn into the looming altercation of words.

"Neither am I," Richard agreed.

Bingley's lips tilted up on one side into a sly smirk. "Then, perhaps, since you are not old and Miss Mary is not too young – that is what you said, is it not, Darcy?"

Darcy shook his head. "Yes, that is what I said but..."

Bingley continued without waiting for Darcy to finish his thought, "Perhaps we can all three be brothers."

"Richard and Miss Mary?"

Bingley shrugged. "Why not? She seems to be made of stern enough stuff to take on a grumbly, not-old, chap like the colonel. I dare say if he barked orders at her, she would serve him up a sermon for his troubles. As would be deserved, I might add."

Darcy looked to Richard for his response, but his cousin was not looking either shocked or affronted. Instead, his brow was furrowed, and his eyes were focused on the ceiling.

"What are you thinking?" Darcy asked cautiously.

"Bingley might actually be clever."

"You are not thinking of marrying Miss Mary to save her from Mr. Collins, are you?"

Richard shook his head. "No, but how long could this fellow be visiting? A week, maybe two – a month at the most. What if it *appeared* like Miss Mary had other prospects?"

"Do you mean one who has an earl as a relation?" Bingley was sitting forward eagerly.

These two and their schemes! They were both far too interested in putting together a stratagem.

"I do think you really might be clever," Richard said with a laugh.

"You cannot play with her heart." Darcy would not allow it, nor could he fathom that his cousin would even consider it.

"No, I would never. However, I could present the idea of a mutually agreeable ruse to Miss Mary tomorrow."

Bingley snorted. "I wish you well with that. I do not think that Miss Mary approves of disguise."

Richard shrugged. "One never knows until one asks."

"You cannot be serious. You are going to ask Miss Mary to let you pretend to court her?" Nothing good could come of such a plan, and Miss Elizabeth would not be pleased to have her sister put in harm's path.

"Oh, but I am."

And he looked it. Darcy knew the set of jaw and intense stare that shouted that Richard's mind could not be changed.

"Then, you must tell Miss Elizabeth first."

His cousin shook his head. "No, I must speak to Miss Mary first."

"But if my relation," Darcy pointed at Richard, "damages Miss Elizabeth's sister's heart, do you think she will be happy to consider me?"

Bingley rose from his place. "That is easily solved. Present your offer to Miss Elizabeth before the colonel speaks to Miss Mary. You know he is not going to be persuaded to do otherwise."

He plucked his coat from the sofa. "I am going to bed, for tomorrow promises to be an exciting day."

He crossed the room to the door. "And I am leaving the door unlocked, so stay here at your own risk of discovery by my sisters." And with that he threw the door open and left without closing the it behind him.

"Then, if you will not tell Miss Elizabeth," Darcy said in a low voice, "I will."

Again, Richard shrugged. "Do what you have to do, but I think you are worried for naught." He rose. "Are you staying here longer?"

"No. I can pace a path in my room behind a locked door while I contemplate things." And there was much to consider.

Could he really ask Miss Elizabeth to consider marrying him if his cousin was playing such a dangerous game? Maybe he should wait until after Mr. Collins left, just in case Richard's plan unravelled in a spectacularly disastrous mess. How would she be able to even bear to be in his presence if his cousin were the cause of one of her sisters' hearts being broken?

Richard stopped at the door to the library and closed it, blocking Darcy's path.

"Just one more thing. I know you are pondering disaster, and I wish you had more faith in my tactical skills. However, I know how you are and am not offended." He paused. "That letter from your father. You know Miss

Elizabeth is the lady who meets all that your father wants you to have in a wife, do you not?"

Darcy nodded.

"Then, in your pondering, ask yourself this: If we are not successful tomorrow and one of her sisters ends up tied to that ne'er-do-well blackguard who broke Georgiana's heart, would that relationship be enough for you to deny your heart and disappoint your father's expectations?"

Well, now, that was a good question.

Chapter 12

ELIZABETH SIGHED WITH PLEASURE as she lifted her face to the sunshine. The air was cool, but the sun was bright and warm.

"It is a gloriously fine day, is it not?" Jane asked.

"It is," Elizabeth agreed. "I hope that our sisters do not dampen the day."

"That is a thought that is not without merit." Jane turned so she could see the front of Netherfield. "I will miss our quiet time here, but I am pleased to be well enough to go home."

"It is not our quiet time you will miss," Elizabeth teased. "And I dare say it will not be overly long until this is your home."

"I do hope you are correct, but I also hope this home does not come with sisters."

Elizabeth giggled. "You know it might, but Mr. Bingley will not tolerate either of his sisters being anything less than all that is polite to you. You have seen how very put out he has been with them for their lies to you."

Jane smiled. "He has been rather wonderful, has he not? I had hoped there was a spark of fierceness behind his amiable façade. Indeed, I had suspected there was, so it is lovely to be correct on that front."

"You thought there was a fierceness to Mr. Bingley?" The idea of such a thing had never once occurred to Elizabeth, and she had always prided herself on being a good judge of character and possessing the ability to discover the secrets that a person might try to hide about themselves.

"Oh, yes. From the first time I met him, I thought it must be so."

Elizabeth shook her head. "I do not see how. He has been pleasantness personified, with a jolly, happy smile nearly always affixed to his visage. What in his manners or expression gave you cause to suspect as you did?"

"Have you learned nothing from being my sister?"

Elizabeth blinked at the question. "I am afraid I do not know how to answer that. I would like to say I have learned a great deal, but from the tone of your voice, it seems I have missed some important lesson."

The door opened behind them.

"It is Mr. Darcy," Jane whispered.

"I do not see how he is the lesson I have missed."

Jane chuckled. "That is not what I meant, and you know it. Although..." her voice trailed off for a moment as her gaze was fixed on the still open door to Netherfield where Mr. Darcy stood with his back to them. "How often do I smile?"

"Nearly always when in public, and nearly as frequently at home unless you are in our room."

"And how often am I wearing a smile when you know I feel like scowling or pouting?"

"I am not sure that I can quantify that." For it happened frequently enough.

"Would you agree that I am not always as calm and happy as I appear by my expression?"

"I would." Elizabeth had seen Jane reply to someone with the utmost civility in public only to hear her grumble loudly about that person, and what she had truly wished to say but knew she should not, once they were safely tucked away at home. In fact, Elizabeth had often envied Jane's ability to hold her tongue.

"Then, you know that how one appears is not precisely how one is."

"Of course, I do, but I still do not know how you managed to suspect Mr. Bingley was anything but pleasant when I did not."

Jane chuckled. "Is your pride hurt?"

"Now is not the time to tease," Elizabeth snapped before smiling sheepishly and adding, "It stings quite sharply. So what was your clue?"

"Mr. Darcy," Jane whispered.

Elizabeth cast a look toward the house, but Mr. Darcy had only turned and was looking somewhat annoyed about something. He caught her eye, smiled, and gave a nod of his head.

"He is the clue," Jane continued.

"He is?" Elizabeth's brow furrowed.

Jane nodded. "I did not think – and still do not think – anyone can be someone who is easily bent if he is the particular friend of such an imposing gentleman as Mr. Darcy, for I do not think Mr. Darcy suffers fools, and a person who sways this way and that is often foolish, for they do not know which way to go unless someone else directs them."

That made sense, but...

"But it seemed to me that Mr. Bingley wished too greatly for his friend's approval."

Jane laughed at that as she shook her head in disagreement. "Do you remember the insult? At the assembly?"

Did Elizabeth remember it? She would likely never forget it!

"Think back to what was said. Surely you heard how Mr. Bingley tormented Mr. Darcy. I saw it from where I was dancing, and from what I saw, it seemed he was not easily put off until what Mr. Darcy said made you scowl. And do you know what Mr. Bingley did then?"

Elizabeth shook her head slowly. She had focused almost completely on the unkind words of the handsome gentleman whom she had hoped would ask her to dance but who had instead proclaimed her unworthy of his attention. Oh, her pride was destined to be trampled on today, was it not?

"Mr. Bingley laughed," Jane said in answer to her own question. "Then, he leaned close to his friend and said something to him that made Mr. Darcy's expression darken, and only then did he leave him standing alone."

Well, that did put a new light on Mr. Bingley.

"You would do well to consider Mr. Darcy," Jane whispered. "I think you two suit each other quite well."

"We argue."

Jane smiled and took Elizabeth's hand. "Of course, you do. You argue with all whose opinion matters to you. Do not deny it, for it is the very reason why you are arguing with me now."

Elizabeth scowled at her sister. Jane had always known her best.

"Smile," Jane hissed. "Your gentleman is about to join us."

"He is not –" A sharp tug on her hand stopped Elizabeth's protest.

"Is anything amiss?" Mr. Darcy asked as he approached them ahead of his cousin and Mr. Bingley. A deep concerned crease sat between his eyebrows as he studied Elizabeth's face. Was it because he thought something was wrong with her?

"Nothing is amiss," Jane answered. "I fear I have been tormenting my sister and made her sunny disposition a touch cloudy."

"Then, you are well?" Mr. Darcy's eyes continued to search Elizabeth's face.

"Yes, I am perfectly well. It is as my sister has said. She is well enough to tease me, so it really is the best day to be going home. You would not wish to host two ladies who were hurling jibes at each other."

"I do not hurl jibes," Jane retorted.

"You see what I mean?" Elizabeth asked with a laugh.

Mr. Darcy's lips curled into a beautiful soft smile as they seemed to always do when he was relaxed and in the company of friends. This was something Elizabeth had learned about him during her sojourn at Netherfield. The gentleman who appeared in an assembly room filled to overflowing with strangers was not the same gentleman who appeared once the doors were closed to public scrutiny.

"I am happy to hear you are both well."

"Was there a fear someone was ill?" Mr. Bingley had just joined them. "You do not have to leave today."

"We must leave," Jane assured him. "Not because we wish to do so," she added. "But I am well, and so is Elizabeth. And there are our younger sisters about whom to think."

"I had not forgotten." Mr. Bingley's smile chased away his look of concern as he extended his hand to Jane. "But I am in no rush to see my guests depart."

"We are going to town and then Longbourn," the colonel said. "It is not as if you are sending them packing to some distant port. It is three miles, is it not?" He looked to Elizabeth.

"Just."

"The day is dwindling." He made a sweeping motion of his hand toward the open carriage door. "And there are villains to roust." He clapped his hands together as if he were eager for the opportunity to *roust the villains*.

"What exactly does rousting entail?" Jane asked cautiously as Mr. Bingley handed her into the carriage.

"Not as much as I would like," the colonel replied.

"We have agreed that it is just going to be making the scoundrel aware of our presence – most especially Richard's – for now." Mr. Darcy held his hand out to Elizabeth.

"Unless he is foolish; then, I might get to call him out or some such thing."

"You would not, would you?" There was near panic in Jane's tone.

"He is teasing," Elizabeth assured her while sending a look at the colonel that asked if she was right in assuming that.

"Duels are not allowed," Mr. Bingley assured Jane as he settled into the carriage ahead of Elizabeth.

"That is unfortunately true. I will ride ahead." Colonel Fitzwilliam gave both Elizabeth and Mr. Darcy a nod and then went to gather his horse from the groom who was holding him behind the carriage.

"I need to speak to you privately at some point," Mr. Darcy whispered.

Elizabeth looked at him with wide eyes. "About what?" There were very few reasons a gentleman usually requested a private conversation with a lady.

"Your sister and my cousin," he said hastily.

"My sister?" Which one? Jane? She glanced toward the carriage.

"Miss Mary."

Elizabeth's attention snapped back to Mr. Darcy. "Why?" She drew the word out as she asked it.

Mr. Darcy sighed. "He has a plan to keep her safe from Mr. Collins."

Elizabeth's left eyebrow arched. "Indeed?"

"Yes." There was a determined set to his jaw.

"And you do not approve?"

"I am not sure that I do. I can see the possibility of it going badly."

"The day is dwindling!" the colonel called from his horse.

"I will tell you about it later unless you do not mind my discussing it with both you and Miss Bennet?"

"And Mr. Bingley?"

"He already knows the plan." Mr. Darcy stepped with her closer to the carriage. "He does not see the danger as I do."

Elizabeth stood next to the step and studied Mr. Darcy's expression. Worry etched his features and hung in his eyes. "What will put you most at ease?"

He smiled. "You are remarkable."

"I do not see how."

"Not everyone knows when I am ill-at-ease."

"While I appreciate the flattery, and I would like to think it is well-deserved, I find that I cannot accept it because your worry is not well-concealed and takes very little to discern." She tipped her head to the side as she smiled at him and had the smile returned.

Jane might be right. Mr. Darcy might be well-suited to her. Not that he would ever consider her as more than a friend. Nor did she want him to – did she? Her heart was not willing to answer that with a ready reply, and she feared it was not only Mary's heart that was in danger of being harmed by one of the gentlemen from Netherfield.

"We will discuss it now if Jane is amenable. It might be best if we both knew of whatever it was your cousin is planning."

"That is a wise choice. I should have considered that myself, but I admit that my concern was only for you."

The comment nearly made Elizabeth stumble as she was climbing into the carriage. His concern was only for her? Did that mean…? No, surely, it was just because they were friends, and he knew how worried she was about her sisters. They shared that character trait. That was all that it was. It surely did not mean he admired her.

"I was beginning to wonder if you were going to join us," Mr. Bingley teased as Mr. Darcy entered the carriage. "We will do well to reach Meryton before the shops are closed."

"We could have been gone sooner if you had not insisted upon writing a reply to that invitation," Mr. Darcy grumbled.

"You cannot put that to my account because I lay the blame for it entirely on my sisters," Mr. Bingley said.

"I do not see how you can. They were nowhere near when we were preparing to depart."

This conversation was one which made it rather clear to Elizabeth how the insult at the assembly had happened just as Jane had said. Mr. Bingley was indeed not one to be put off easily. She supposed that was a good thing – at least, sometimes.

"They were the ones – Louisa in particular – who attempted to keep the invitation from me. I was fortunate to have discovered their ploy this morning. I really could not wait to make my reply. They need to know that I am going to settle into the community and will welcome Miss Bennet and her family no matter how they feel about it."

"May I ask what invitation you nearly did not receive?" Jane's voice was nearly a whisper.

Mr. Bingley's attention was immediately given to her. It was a sight that pleased Elizabeth's heart while at the same time made it pang with longing to be so doted on as her sister was.

"Mr. and Mrs. Philips have invited us to a dinner party tomorrow evening. I have happily accepted on the behalf of myself, the colonel, and Darcy. I told my sisters they would have to send their own regrets or acceptance."

"I suspect that Hurst will do the replying," Mr. Darcy added.

"I think you are correct. He is as put out with them as I am, so I also expect to see them all in attendance tomorrow evening."

"Should I feel guilty that I have caused strife in your family?" Jane asked.

"You? You have not caused strife!" Mr. Bingley cried. "The ill that was done, was done by my sisters. I am grieved that they have been so calculating. Think no more of it, my dear. They have behaved badly and must deal with the consequences of doing so." This was said with all seriousness and a grave expression, but as soon as the matter had been concluded, Mr. Bingley's regular open expression returned.

"Now, what had you dragging your feet this morning, Darcy? You were rather impatient until we joined the ladies."

Mr. Darcy looked at Elizabeth. "There is a matter I wished to discuss with Miss Elizabeth, and upon consultation with her, it has been decided that what I have to say should also be shared with Miss Bennet."

Mr. Bingley's brow furrowed in confusion. "What matter is that?"

"It is my fear regarding my cousin's plans concerning Miss Mary."

Chapter 13

As the carriage lurched forward, setting Darcy and his companions on their journey to Meryton, Bingley sighed a longsuffering sigh such as Darcy often heard when his friend was exasperated with Darcy's cautious nature.

"I do not know why you are so worried about Richard and Miss Mary," Bingley said. "Miss Mary is capable of making her own decisions, is she not?" He did not pause to give anyone a chance to reply, for who would answer such a question with anything but *yes*? "The colonel will make his request, and she will reply." He shrugged. "I truly do not see how that could go wrong."

"What request is the colonel planning to make?" Miss Bennet asked before Darcy could start to lay out his case for potential disaster.

It was likely best that she had spoken first, however, since Darcy knew that Bingley would hang on every word that fell from Miss Bennet's lips, while Darcy's concerns would be much easier to brush aside.

"Colonel Fitzwilliam thinks a pretended courtship with Miss Mary or a marked attention to her that hinted at a possible courtship would put your mother on the path of discouraging Mr. Collins' suit," Bingley replied.

"A pretend what?" Miss Elizabeth demanded as Miss Bennet blinked in surprise to Bingley's reply.

"Courtship?"

Darcy smiled at his friend's wary tone while, at the same time, he worried that Miss Elizabeth's quick response meant the idea was just as dreadful as he thought it was.

"It will not be feigned if Miss Mary does not give her consent," Bingley added.

"I am not sure that sounds like the best plan." Miss Bennet shared a concerned look with her sister.

"It does not?" Bingley questioned. "How could it not be? Truly. I do not know."

"Let me see if I have the idea of this plan correct," Miss Elizabeth began with a gentle smile that was not altogether happy. "The colonel – a handsome gentleman with a compelling air about him and a family name that is noteworthy – in other words, a marvelous match if a lady should be so fortunate as to snare him."

Here she looked at Miss Bennet who nodded and said, "Oh to be sure. There are no better credentials to recommend a gentleman to a lady than those the colonel possesses except if he were his older brother and had a title himself."

That response brought a genuine smile to Miss Elizabeth's lips and, despite the praise of his cousin's potential as a suitor causing him some unease, Darcy sat back and allowed Miss Elizabeth to point out to his friend the folly in thinking that Richard's plan was wonderful. It was delightful to consider that, should he be successful in winning her good opinion and her hand, he would have such an able partner in all areas of life. However, a niggling worry scampered its way through his mind that should Richard not listen to reason, Darcy's ability to secure Miss Elizabeth as his wife would be greatly reduced.

"To continue, this paragon of potential husbands, who I am sure is sought after by many, plans to say to my sister – perhaps not in these words, but the meaning will carry – I was wondering if you would allow me to protect you from the gentleman whom you do not want to marry but who seems to want to marry you, but please allow your mind to rest easy as I have no interest in you in that sense. It is only a ruse. Nothing more."

"And this is a problem?"

"Yes!" Miss Elizabeth answered.

"I do not see how. Is it not best to have all the facts presented at the start?"

Miss Elizabeth sighed. "I will allow that honesty is an admirable thing, but do try to imagine how a young lady might feel upon being told she is not the sort of lady who could possibly capture in reality the interest of a gentleman like the colonel – *by the colonel*."

She peeked at Darcy as she said that part.

"Much like my words at the assembly?" The weight of that poor decision fell heavy on Darcy anew.

One shoulder lifted and lowered in reluctant response. "It can be hurtful."

And, Darcy knew that it could break the heart of not only the lady, but also the gentleman, when he realized what he had truly done. Much as her soft answer had just done to his heart.

"Apologies can be made." He held her gaze as he spoke. "But the damage will be done." And could linger.

She drew the corner of her bottom lip between her teeth as she gave a small nod of agreement.

"If I could go back…"

She smiled and shook her head. "I know."

Darcy turned to Bingley. "Do you now see the potential for disaster? No lady wants to be made to feel as if they are lacking – especially when they clearly are not. Miss Mary is a lovely young woman. I would hate to see her heart hurt."

When he turned back to Miss Elizabeth, after Bingley had, somewhat reluctantly, agreed that the plan was not without some danger, she was looking at him curiously.

"Have I said something amiss?"

"No. I think we agree perfectly on why your cousin's plan is not a good one, but do you truly believe my sister is not lacking?"

Darcy shrugged. "I cannot think of a way she is lacking."

Miss Elizabeth's left eyebrow arched.

"I speak the truth from what I know about her. I suppose I may find some small area that needs improvement upon better acquaintance."

"Would you, then, be happy to see her with your cousin?"

From Miss Elizabeth's expression there seemed to be something of great importance that lay behind her query.

"I think she may be a trifle young, but that is no fault of her own or to her discredit. Is there a reason you think that she would not be a good choice for Richard? You know her far better than I do."

"I think they would make a lovely pair," Bingley inserted.

"Do you?" Miss Bennet asked.

"Without a doubt. Your sister seems to possess a sternness of spirit that would match well with the colonel's demanding nature."

"Her heart is not made of stone," Miss Elizabeth cautioned.

"I do not mean that the colonel is a tyrant or would do anything to injure the heart of another for whom he cared. It is just that he is used to getting his way in all things, and occasionally, he needs someone as resolute as Darcy to challenge him on a plan and to hand him no sympathy at all when he proceeds and is unsuccessful." Bingley shook his head. "Much like I do. I admit to you freely and to my shame that I can be as exuberant about a scheme as Richard is sure. It was only Darcy who balked at the idea of a feigned courtship when it was brought forward. Thankfully, I am more easily swayed from my exuberance than Richard is from a campaign."

"Then, what are we to do about the colonel and Mary?" Miss Bennet asked. "I will admit that she is several years younger than the colonel, but I have seen matches with more years separating husband and wife that have been beautiful and lasting." She peeked at her sister. "I think they pair well, but that is not necessarily a good thing in this situation. Nor is it a reason to promote the colonel's plan. What if it were to happen that one should love the other? Then, this scheme could pose an impediment of great significance in seeing them happily matched. For who would believe that a lie was not actually a lie but rather the truth that was not known? There must be something better that can be done to see both of them happy."

Oh, dear! Darcy's mind rang in alarm at Miss Bennet's eager tone. Bingley, who liked to dabble in attempting to guess who would do well with whom, was about to tie himself to a lady who seemed happy to contemplate the same topics. Of course, Darcy had to admit that he thought Miss Bennet likely thought more deeply about the possible outcomes than Bingley did, which, he reluctantly supposed, would make for a good alliance.

"Matchmaking is never without its dangers," he cautioned. "That is why I do not partake in the sport."

"I am not saying we should push them together." Miss Bennet hurried to assure him. "However, I would not refrain from encouraging one with a good word about the other." Her eyes flicked briefly in her sister's direction before returning to his. "Be that as it may, it is not for me to decide the matter. That must be agreed upon between the happy couple if they are to be happy at all."

"What Jane says is true. If by chance either Mary or the colonel admired the other as more than just an acquaintance, this plan could..." She finished her thought with a simple shake of her head.

"Are you saying?" Miss Bennet asked her.

A pained expression accompanied Miss Elizabeth's small nod.

"Does your sister admire my cousin?" Darcy asked it in a whisper though there was no reason to keep anyone from hearing him. It just seemed that such an inquiry should be done gently.

"I think she might. I saw the way she looked at him at breakfast that morning."

"Well, that does complicate things even more, does it not?" Bingley said.

Indeed, it did, for it meant that there was little chance that Miss Mary's heart would not be scarred.

"We should stop the carriage and tell Richard he cannot present his offer to your sister," Mr. Bingley said with no little amount of conviction.

"No!" Miss Elizabeth cried. "He cannot know that she might admire him. I do not know for certain, but if it is true, then she would be mortified to have him know – especially since he does not return her regard."

"Then, what do we do?" There was a note of desperation in Miss Bennet's question.

"We stop the carriage and tell him that we are agreed that it is a dangerous thing to do as he plans." Bingley rapped on the ceiling and the carriage began to slow immediately. "Leave it to me. All will be well."

Miss Elizabeth cast a worried look at Darcy who could only shrug in response. He knew Bingley was adept at talking around a situation, but there was the chance that more could be revealed than anyone would like.

Bingley poked his head out of the window. "Colonel, we have need of you," he called and then, relaxed back into his seat.

"How may I be of service?" The colonel asked when he appeared at the side of the carriage.

"Your plan has a flaw."

"I beg your pardon?"

"Darcy has explained your plan to Miss Elizabeth and Miss Bennet, and it has been decided that it is not a scheme without the possibility of doing great harm to Miss Mary. We are all in agreement."

The colonel looked at each occupant of the vehicle. "You all think I am wrong?"

"Only because you are so wonderful," Bingley answered.

Richard laughed. "Is that right?"

"It has been brought to my attention, that if I were a young miss and if I were to be told that I was not good enough to be anything more than a charity case, it would be devastating," Bingley said.

Richard shook his head. "I do not understand how. I plan to ask Miss Mary if she would like my help in fending off the unwanted attention of Mr. Collins. How does that make her an unwanted charity case?"

"She is a lady." Bingley folded his arms across his chest and sat back as if that statement answered everything.

"I am aware of that. She is a lady who does not want Mr. Collins to press his suit with her."

Bingley held up a cautionary finger to punctuate what he was about to say. "She will hear it as if you are saying she is not good enough for anyone as wonderful as you – Miss Elizabeth and Miss Bennet both assure me that you are a fine catch."

Again, Richard shook his head. "I will not harm her heart. I would never do such a thing."

"You cannot guarantee that her heart will not be hurt," Darcy inserted. "You can only control the things that are within your power, and what happens in Miss Mary's heart or head are not within that realm."

"I will bear the guilt if anything goes awry. It will be my fault and mine alone."

"And who will care for my sister?" Miss Elizabeth gave him a steely look.

"She needs someone to act as a buffer between her and your cousin."

Miss Elizabeth did not flinch from staring him down.

"We will meet them." Richard used his most cajoling tone, which did nothing to change Miss Elizabeth's expression. "And if this Collins fellow is as dreadful as he sounded to be in Miss Mary's letter, I will offer my services. It is not in me to stand by and observe when I know that I can provide protection. It is why I have worn the uniform I have worn, and it is why I am looking to parliament for my next area of service."

Miss Elizabeth's head tilted, and her expression softened just a bit. "I imagine that while your uniform is a welcome sight to many, it also draws enemies and their anger."

"That it does."

Her lips curled into a smile. "I would rather remain friends than become enemies, so proceed with caution, Colonel."

He touched his hat and nodded. "I would not wish to lose something so precious as your friendship. I will heed your warning."

"Thank you."

"Promise me one thing, Miss Elizabeth."

"What is that, Colonel?"

"If my campaign does not succeed, allow me to be the only casualty who must fall. Do not cast aside my friend or my cousin on account of my failure."

She looked at Darcy and then Bingley and again at Darcy before nodding. "I promise."

"I will do my best to be a success."

Darcy watched Miss Elizabeth in silence for a minute as they resumed their journey.

"Is there yet something troubling you?" she asked.

Could he – should he – reveal his heart to her? He glanced at his friend and her sister and shrugged without thought. It was how he felt – unsure, conflicted, longing to say something, and yet not wishing to say anything at all.

"You do not have to tell me." Her whisper was barely audible.

He could just let the topic fade into the air surrounding them, but that seemed the cowardly thing to do.

Therefore, he took a breath and began the confession that promised to either give him hope or dash any hope he had to bits.

"I was merely wondering if you could keep the promise you made to my cousin. I would struggle with it if it were me whose sister was being placed in harm's way. I..." He swallowed. "What if the sight of anyone connected to my cousin caused Miss Mary to feel the pain all over again? How could you keep me as a friend, let alone as anything more?"

There. It was done. His heart had been revealed. Now, all there was to do was wait until the wide-eyed look of shock faded from her face and she could answer him.

Chapter 14

ANYTHING MORE?

Elizabeth could not pull her eyes away from Mr. Darcy. Had he truly just implied that he would like to court her?

Her? The lady whom he had called only tolerable two months ago?

She squeezed her eyes closed. Surely, she must have misheard him. But what if she had not? How was she to answer him? She opened her eyes and saw him still looking at her as if he truly did expect a reply.

Jane nudged her, and when Elizabeth looked at her sister, she saw that Jane was wearing a delighted smile.

That confirmed it. Mr. Darcy had said what she thought he had said.

"Are you proposing a courtship?" she asked just to make sure she was correct in her thinking. It seemed poor form to proceed without knowing with absolute clarity what was being discussed.

His steady gaze did not waver. "Not exactly, though that should come first."

Elizabeth's eyes grew as wide as they could. "Marriage?" she forced the startling word over her dry tongue and out of her mouth.

"Yes, eventually."

Her brow furrowed. "Are you mad?" She pressed her lips together. "I apologize. That was to remain in my mind."

Mr. Bingley's chuckling was interrupted by a snort. She shot him a look of displeasure, to which his only reply was to hold up the one hand that was not covering his mouth as if that gesture was some sort of apology.

"Perhaps I am mad," Mr. Darcy said. "I have thought myself so and even asked my cousin if it were too soon to be considering you as my wife, but to even think that you might accept someone else or that some other gentleman might offer for you..." He stopped speaking and his cheeks puffed out before he expelled a breath. "I am making a hash of this, am I not?"

"Well, admitting you thought ... yourself mad ... to be considering her as a wife ... is not perhaps the best way to present yourself." Mr. Bingley's answer to the question that Mr. Darcy had posed to Elizabeth was punctuated throughout and followed by laughter.

"That is not what I meant!" Mr. Darcy's face was growing quite red. "It is just that two months seemed too short an acquaintance upon which to base such a monumental decision, and yet, to consider any other option seems impossible to do. I assure you that I am not normally someone who makes hasty choices."

"But sometimes one knows immediately what the best course of action is, and no amount of dithering back and forth will ever change what is right from being what is right," Jane said. "Would you not agree, Elizabeth? Is it not similar to how quickly I found my heart lost to Mr. Bingley? It was *you* who encouraged me that it was not too fast a thing to have happen."

Of course, her sister would remember that and draw a very good comparison. "But Mr. Bingley has always found you..." She glanced at Mr. Darcy. How did she say this? Appealing? Tempting? Beautiful?

"More than tolerable." That seemed safest.

Jane took Elizabeth's hand. "This is precisely why the colonel's idea is not a good one." She cast a look at Mr. Bingley. "Do you understand now?" she asked him.

His laughter had ceased. "Oh, most clearly," he assured her. "Darcy was merely trying to be rid of me," he assured Elizabeth. "He is not so deficient as to truly think of you as anything less than lovely."

"That is true, and we have discussed this," Mr. Darcy inserted and then sighed. "Allow me to try to explain myself, and hopefully better than I have done thus far." He looked at Elizabeth with such earnest need that she could reply in no other way than to allow him the chance for which he wished.

"You have captured my interest for some time now, and it is true that I find you lovely – bewitching even. However, it was my father's description of you that forced me to realize what my heart already knew. You are who I desire and, yes, even need."

The bewitching part of his explanation was lovely; the being needed and desired was gratifying; the rest, however, was rather confusing. "Your father's description convinced you? How is that possible since I have not even met your father?"

"His final letter to me." Mr. Darcy fished the missive out of the pocket of his greatcoat. "You may read it if you wish. His description of whom he would accept as my wife is you. There is only one qualification that I cannot say if you meet or not, for it is only something you can answer, and I fear we have not had enough time together yet for you to answer it as I long for you to do." His cheeks puffed out again before he released a breath as Elizabeth took the letter from him. "You do not have to read it now. We are nearly to town."

"I am too curious to wait." She gave him what she hoped was an encouraging smile. He seemed so ill-at-ease. To think that her good opinion mattered so much to him as to make him look like he might become ill was... well, it was rather endearing. How could she not feel the honour he bestowed upon her?

"May I also read it?" Jane asked.

Mr. Darcy only nodded.

Elizabeth's eyes drank in the words on the page, causing her mind to conjure a picture of the elder Mr. Darcy in her mind, and she had to admit that she likely would have liked him had she ever met him. She peeked at Mr. Darcy. "Are you like your father?" she asked before she continued reading.

"Yes," Mr. Bingley answered.

"I have been told I am," Mr. Darcy said. "I suppose I see it to a degree."

"He sounds lovely. It is no small compliment to my sister to say that these things describe her." Jane pointed to the words on the page.

Elizabeth pushed her hand away. She could see the words and had read them three times already.

"And yet, they are likely too small to do her justice," Mr. Darcy replied.

Elizabeth felt as if her cheeks were going to burst into flames. "You truly think so highly of me?"

"I do."

"You love me?"

"Most ardently." He shook his head as if that fact befuddled him.

Elizabeth bit her lip and studied his face. There was no twitch of his lips or teasing twinkle in his eye. He genuinely did look serious. Was this something she wanted? Was *he* who she wanted? There was, she supposed, only one way to discover the truth.

"Very well," she said as she folded the letter. "You may court me while I discover if I can love you in return." She held the letter out to him. His soft smile, such as he wore now, was something about him that she could already say she loved. "You are not just doing this to protect me from Mr. Collins, are you?"

Mr. Darcy's smile faded. "No, I assure you I am not. However, I will admit that I am perhaps presenting my offer sooner than I might have had the threat of his attempting to court you not been present."

Her eyes narrowed. So, was that a good thing or not?

"I am a selfish creature, Miss Elizabeth. I promise I am not trying to save you from an unwanted suitor for your sake but for my own." He placed the letter in his pocket. "About my cousin and Miss Mary..."

"I suggest that you deal with it if or when it happens," Jane inserted quietly.

"I would second that," Mr. Bingley said with a broad grin.

Elizabeth sighed silently. Having Jane gently, in her too much like Mama but with a softer touch manner, nudging her toward Mr. Darcy was bad enough. She did not need to have Mr. Bingley doing so as well.

"That does seem to be the most logical way to proceed," she agreed.

"Do you wish for this?" Mr. Darcy motioned between himself and her. "You are not just accepting me to spare my feelings because we have an audience?" His hands rubbed circles on his knees.

"I do wish for this." There was more she might have said: She had found him handsome from the moment she saw him and had, since his apology, found her mind filled with thoughts of him. He intrigued her, and courting him felt right, as if it were the most natural thing in the world, which was both a wonderful and an unsettling feeling. But they did have an audience.

The carriage began to slow.

"Then, may I speak to your father to tell him my intentions?"

"You may."

Mr. Bingley clapped his hands together. "Capital! And I must extend my best wishes to you Miss Elizabeth." Then, he turned to Darcy. "We can approach Mr. Bennet together."

That seemed to cause Mr. Darcy to look a trifle less nervous – but only a trifle.

"However," Mr. Bingley continued, "first, we must meet this Collins fellow and see to Wickham."

Jane leaned toward the window. "My sisters are where I told Mary we would meet them, and the colonel has just joined them." She pulled Elizabeth closer and pointed to the group in front of the milliner's shop. "If that is Mr. Wickham, I can see why he is successful with the ladies," she whispered.

"He is handsome even from a distance," Elizabeth agreed.

"But his comeliness is only a shallow façade if it is not more superficial than that," Mr. Darcy muttered.

The carriage rolled to a stop.

"Mr. Wickham does not look pleased to see your cousin," Jane said with a giggle.

"Oh, I am sure he is not," Mr. Darcy agreed. "Shall we also make ourselves known to him?"

The door next to him was open, and the steps were in place, so he exited and extended his hand to help Elizabeth from the carriage.

"Darcy!" Richard said in welcome. "You will never believe who is here."

Mr. Darcy did not release Elizabeth's hand when she had gained the ground, but instead, he wrapped her arm around his and held her hand in place near his elbow.

"Wickham." The greeting given by Mr. Darcy was more of a rumble than a word.

Elizabeth could feel the tension in the small area of Mr. Darcy's person that lay under her hand. She could not blame him for how he was presenting himself. She was certain she would not be so well regulated as he if it were her greeting a former friend who had betrayed her and harmed her sister.

"Oh, Mr. Darcy." A large gentleman, wearing a jacket the colour of a cleric's robe, stumbled forward and bowed low. "I have heard so much about you. It is an honour to make your acquaintance. It is a kind thing that you do, offering to drive my cousins to town."

"Who are you?"

Elizabeth pressed her lips together to keep her amusement contained at the imperious tone Mr. Darcy used. He knew who had approached him, and the man seemed as ridiculous as Mary's description.

"My apologies. I am Mr. Collins." He bowed low once again. "I am your esteemed aunt's parson."

"Ah, I see." Mr. Darcy turned away from Mr. Collins and toward his cousin. "Have you met my cousin?" he asked with a glance toward Mr. Collins. "This is Colonel Richard Fitzwilliam."

Mr. Collins gave a little gasp. "Fitzwilliam, you say?"

"Yes."

"And he is your cousin, you say?"

"His father, the earl, is Lady Catherine's brother."

"The earl." The words were whispered in awe.

"Cousin," Mr. Darcy continued, "this is Mr. Collins, who I gather is a cousin of some sort to the Bennets."

"My father was their father's cousin," Mr. Collins inserted.

"And you are my aunt's parson?" the colonel asked.

"Oh, yes, recently installed at Hunsford. It is a delightful parish, and your aunt has been very generous."

"My aunt?" the colonel said with a laugh. "You should likely brush up on the meaning of generous if she is your idea of what it is."

Something flashed in the colonel's eyes, and his lips curled into a sly smile. "You may be of use to Mr. Wickham."

"Indeed?" Mr. Collins had moved from next to Darcy to a position much closer to the son of the earl.

Some people were so easily swayed by a person's position and connections. She glanced at the man on whose arm her hand rested. How often did he face such fawning? She supposed it was constant. After all, the first thing she had known about him was that he was wealthy – the sort of gentleman everyone wished to count as their friend and have marry their daughter.

"Yes," the colonel was saying, "he at one point was destined to take orders, though at first, he thought the law might be better suited to him. It might be possible that you could help him decide now whether his chosen profession is for him, or if, perchance, he was too quick in giving up his pursuit of becoming a man of the cloth."

"There is no need for assistance," Mr. Wickham said. "I do not think I am suited to the church."

"But are you certain?" Mr. Collins asked. "One should not walk outside the will of the Lord. You have only to look at –"

"I am certain," Mr. Wickham inserted before casting a glare in the colonel's direction. "Last year, I was hopeful of marrying well, but the lady proved untrustworthy."

"Is that so?" the colonel stepped closer to Mr. Wickham. "Tread carefully." There was a rather menacing growl to the softly spoken words.

Elizabeth looked in Mary's direction. She was smiling at the colonel in the way one does when enamoured with a gentleman. "Mary," Elizabeth said. "Who are your acquaintances?"

Mary turned her attention to Elizabeth. "Do you wish for me to make the introductions?"

"I would indeed." And not just because Elizabeth wanted to know each person's name, but also because it might just prevent an altercation in the street.

Chapter 15

"Miss Bennet, Miss Elizabeth." Wickham, upon the conclusion of Miss Mary's introduction, gave Darcy a taunting look as he bowed neatly to the two new-to-him Bennet ladies. That look was a sure sign that he was planning to charm them away from Darcy, for it was not the first time he had seen it on his former friend's face.

"It is a pleasure to meet you both," the man continued. "Your sisters have been sharing their purchases with me while waiting for you to arrive."

"Sharing your purchases? Have they already been made when you were to wait for us?" Miss Bennet gave her youngest sister a stern look.

"It was far too tempting!" Miss Lydia cried.

Then, she did something that made Darcy's jaw clench. She fluttered her lashes at Wickham.

"Do not worry, dear Jane," she continued sweetly. "We have made the best selection. Mr. Wickham assures me it is true."

"Best selection or not, you were to wait so that we could coordinate our purchases," Miss Bennet scolded.

"I had no idea that my advice would cause you distress. I do apologize." The placating smile Wickham offered Miss Bennet made Darcy draw in a silent, hopefully, calming breath. The cad likely knew very well what he was doing.

"Did no one tell you that they were to *wait for their sisters*?" Miss Bennet sent another harsh scowl at Lydia before arching a questioning brow in Mary's direction.

"I tried," Mary muttered.

Apparently, there truly was much more to Miss Bennet than her pleasant smile. Not that Darcy was overly surprised by that fact any longer – not since that morning in the breakfast room when she had challenged Miss Bingley and made her intentions regarding his friend known. Still, it was comforting to Darcy to know that his friend would be marrying someone with the ability to be unpleasant when necessary.

"And I did stop her from allowing him to purchase them for her," Mary whispered.

Darcy glared at Wickham. It was just the sort of thing the scoundrel did. He would buy a few pretty baubles to entice the ladies and then, speak sweetly to them until they believed he was in truth as good as he appeared.

"Are you actually in funds?" Richard inserted himself into the conversation before Wickham could once again beg forgiveness for being unaware of what he chose to ignore.

"I do not see how that is any business of yours." Wickham's tone was sharp and cold.

It was truly amazing how his cousin could make Wickham's charm scatter like ashes in a stiff breeze.

"I think it would be best if we spoke of something less personal on the street," Mr. Collins inserted before following it with a "that is if the colonel and Mr. Darcy are in agreement" and a shallow bow that looked a bit like a curtsey. It was rather graceful looking for a man of his size.

He was an odd fellow. Darcy could see why Miss Mary would not wish to be tied to him. However, the man had a point.

"I think that is an excellent idea," Darcy agreed before Richard could say anything else.

His cousin did not care if he ended up brawling with Wickham on the street. Darcy could see it in his tense stance. Of course, Darcy could not blame him for wanting to lay his hands on the man since Wickham had mentioned Georgiana.

"I most heartily agree, so if you would be so kind as to accept our pleasure at having met and allow us to move on with our plans," Miss Elizabeth said, "we really do need to get our shopping done so that we can return home."

Darcy took one step towards the door with her.

"Come along," Miss Elizabeth said to her younger sisters.

"There is no need for we are already done," Miss Lydia declared. "We will wait here for you."

"No, you will not." Miss Elizabeth removed her hand from Darcy's arm and turned toward her youngest sister.

"I do not see why I cannot stay here."

Darcy braced himself for the argument that looked like it was brewing in Miss Lydia's thunderous expression.

Miss Elizabeth smiled. Why was she smiling? He would not be if faced with a recalcitrant sister.

"My dearest Lydia," she said in a sweet, cajoling sort of tone, "staying here would court disaster."

Darcy could not agree with that more!

"What if I purchase the same ribbon you did?" Miss Elizabeth continued. "Our dress and hair might match. Are you willing to take that chance?"

Darcy's lips turned up slightly. That was not the disaster he was imagining, but it was one which he supposed would be beyond horrible to Miss Lydia.

"You can take our parcel," Miss Lydia offered.

To Darcy's surprise, Miss Elizabeth accepted the bundle of goods wrapped in paper and string. What was she doing? Was she truly going to allow her sister to spend more time with Wickham?

"That is an excellent idea. It will make it so much easier for me to return what you have selected and replace it if I decide I like it better."

She looked at Darcy and tipped her head toward the store. He offered her his arm, and they moved swiftly through the shop's door, which was being held open by a footman.

Miss Lydia scampered after them. "Wait! I want to keep those."

"That was very cleverly done," Darcy whispered.

"Thank you. It is not the first time I have dealt with an obstinate sister."

"I want my parcel!" Miss Lydia demanded.

"When we are through," Miss Bennet caught Miss Lydia's hand. "Join me and Mr. Bingley."

Miss Lydia huffed.

"I am quite excited to know what you have chosen for the ball," Bingley said.

Miss Elizabeth looked at Darcy in surprise. "Is he really?" she whispered as they took a few steps away from Miss Bennet and Miss Lydia.

"No, I dare say he is just trying to charm your sister."

"Which one?" Miss Elizabeth asked.

"I suspect both," Darcy replied with a chuckle. Bingley excelled as much at smoothing over awkward situations as he was known for creating them. Most often, those awkward situations came to be when he was taunting Darcy.

Miss Elizabeth laughed. "And are you at all interested in seeing what we purchase?"

"Not a whit," Darcy answered honestly, "though I will appreciate it greatly when I see it adorning your person at Bingley's ball."

Darcy possessed precisely no ability to envision how divine this lace or that ribbon would look on a particular dress or bonnet. His sister and aunt had attempted for years to get him to imagine such things, but he could not. He preferred to see the ensemble once it was completed rather than when it was still bits and pieces.

"Then, would you prefer to wait for us outside?" Miss Elizabeth offered.

It was an offer he would have gladly taken had he been accompanying his aunt and sister. However, today, he had no desire to wait outside or in the carriage, nor, had there been no Wickham or Mr. Collins to worry about, would he have stayed home to avoid accompanying Miss Elizabeth into this shop.

He shook his head. "Strangely, no. I am quite content to stay here and readily admit to being a trifle fascinated to see you make your selections."

"I am certain your sister has made similar choices. It cannot be too novel a thing."

"My sister is not you." He lowered his voice. "I love her in a completely different way."

She pressed her lips together as she indicated to a clerk the tray of lace that she wished to look at more closely. "Are you flirting with me, Mr. Darcy?"

"Is declaring the truth flirting? For that is all I was doing."

She shook her head and chuckled softly as she picked up a length of lace and held it out. "What do you think of this?" Her lips were curled into a most becoming, teasing smile.

"It is lace, and it looks to be well-made," Darcy answered.

"You will have to pardon my friend," Mr. Bingley said. "He is not well-versed in ribbons and lace."

Her lips twitched as if she were attempting to contain a laugh, and there was a laughing quality to her reply to Bingley's words. "Then, let me rephrase my question, sir. Do you find the pattern interesting?"

"I suppose it is, though I am not sure it is any more interesting than any of the others," Darcy replied lightly. There was a wonderfully joyous bubbling that her twinkling eyes stirred inside him.

"That is the one I bought!" Lydia cried as she snatched it from Elizabeth. "Choose another, and why do you care if Mr. Darcy likes the lace you purchase?"

"It is a good thing you were here to stop me from getting this lace," was all Miss Elizabeth answered before picking up a second piece of lace. "I think I like this one better." She shared a secret look with Darcy.

Had she chosen the first lace on purpose? Is that what that sidewards glance and slight arch of her brow were supposed to mean?

"I do not," Miss Lydia muttered.

"Then, it is good that it is for Elizabeth and not for you," Miss Bennet said.

Miss Elizabeth held the second bit of lace so that Darcy could see it better. "See how this one has a less floral pattern than the other?" she asked as, to her right, Bingley exclaimed over the lace that Miss Lydia had purchased.

Darcy nodded. This one did have flowers, but they were scattered and not as plentiful.

"That is why Lydia prefers the other one. She would wear flowers from head to toe every day if she could. I prefer a few blossoms but would rather not be a full bouquet."

Darcy cast a glance at Miss Lydia who was still engaged in a discussion about lace with Bingley. "Then, you chose the other one to prove your point about you sister's need to attend you?'

Miss Elizabeth lifted and lowered one shoulder and smiled in response.

"You are very clever," Darcy whispered. "And I do like this lace better. It looks like something my aunt would wear, and Lady Matlock is always elegantly attired for a soiree."

"She has been known to turn a few heads," Richard inserted. He had been hovering at the edge of the group, moving from side to side, and keeping an eye on the door. "Of course, the only head she truly wishes to turn is that of my father."

"That is lovely," Miss Elizabeth said.

"Is that why you want to know what Mr. Darcy thinks of your lace?" Miss Lydia demanded. Apparently, she had concluded her instruction to Bingley about why her lace was best. "Do you wish to turn his head?"

"She already has," Richard whispered, causing Miss Lydia to gasp, and Miss Elizabeth to sigh.

"Is it true?" Miss Kitty whispered.

"Yes," Darcy answered. There was no need to deny it. He was, after all, going to speak to her father about a courtship later.

"Mama will be delighted," Miss Mary said.

"Oh, indeed!" Miss Lydia cried.

"What is this?" Mr. Collins asked. "What has my cousin done?"

"She has secured Mr. Darcy," Miss Lydia replied. "And if Kitty and I are so fortunate this evening, it will only be Mary who is left without a gentleman."

"You cannot mean..." Miss Bennet began but her question was interrupted by Mr. Collins.

"That cannot be," he said. "I did not know it was Mr. Darcy whom your mother hinted at for your sister, but I assure you it cannot be."

"Why ever not?" Miss Lydia demanded.

"He is promised to another," Mr. Collins answered.

"Oh, for the love of tea and toast!" Richard cried. "Is our aunt still set on that?"

Mr. Collins's shoulders curled forward as if he were trying to shrink into himself.

"What is he talking about?" Miss Bennet asked.

"Our aunt, Lady Catherine, has been set on the notion that her daughter and Darcy would marry since they were children," Richard explained. "My father says it is not to be, as did Darcy's father, yet, Aunt Catherine believes it to be an all but settled event."

"Are you promised to her?" Miss Elizabeth asked quietly.

"No," Darcy replied. "I am free to choose whom I will. You saw my father's wishes." She had read the letter. "If I were promised to another, he would not have given me instructions about what to look for in a wife, and while I love my cousin dearly as one does a cousin, I do not love her as a husband should love his wife." He felt heat rising above his collar and spreading to his ears and cheeks. "Not as my father instructed, and not as I do you."

There was a loud inhale next to him, and Miss Lydia's small hand grasped his free arm.

"Are you going to marry her?" Miss Lydia's excited whisper was loud.

Darcy glanced her direction and noted how there were three clerks attempting to look as if they were not listening, though they clearly were. This conversation was going to be spread from one end of Meryton to the other before the sun had finished its short circuit of the winter sky.

"That has not been determined."

"Oh, can you not see it, Kitty. Jane and Lizzy and you and me, all married."

"None of us are even betrothed, and I do not know who you would be expecting to marry." Miss Bennet's tone was somber. "I know it cannot be the officers we met, for you have not known them long enough to discover their character."

"But they are so handsome!"

"Do you remember what Miss Bingley said at breakfast about not even entertaining the thought of courting a scoundrel?" Richard asked Miss Lydia, who nodded.

"Scoundrels are sometimes quite handsome," he added. "Take care."

"You cannot mean Mr. Wickham?" Her hand flew to her heart. "He does not seem at all like a scoundrel."

"That is precisely how a scoundrel appears," Miss Mary inserted. "I am certain they could not get away with any of the sins they commit if they appeared to be anything less than charming and amiable."

"Miss Mary is correct," the colonel said as he offered her his arm. "That is precisely how he has managed to do the damage I know he has done."

Miss Lydia's eyes were wide. "But he is so handsome," she said sadly.

"There will be other handsome gentlemen who will want to call on you," Darcy said. "You are young. There is no need to determine your destiny today. Give it time."

"But..." Disappointment hung like a thick fog in Miss Lydia's countenance.

"Perhaps you can visit us in town during the season," Richard offered. "I am certain my mother would know of a few eligible, non-scoundrel sorts of gentlemen who might suit."

"Do you mean it?" The fog of disappointment had lifted, and Miss Lydia was once again beaming.

"I will have to speak to your mother and mine before anything can be settled, but I do not see why something cannot be arranged." He glanced at Mr. Collins. "She might even have some suggestions about who might make a good parson's wife."

"But Lady Catherine..."

"Would be pleased to see you well-matched." Richard concluded the man's sentence for him. "Now, Miss Mary, while your older sisters make their selections, perhaps you and your younger sisters could show me which ribbons you chose."

"That should make it so that his plan is not necessary," Miss Bennet whispered to Miss Elizabeth once the younger Bennets had moved to display of ribbons.

Darcy sighed with relief. It appeared as if Miss Elizbeth's heart could rest easy where her sisters were concerned, which in turn, put his own heart at ease and gave it hope that his future happiness would not be tainted by any form of sisterly sorrow.

Chapter 16

ELIZABETH SETTLED INTO A chair in her aunt's sitting room and tried to find a few moments of peace before the onslaught of her aunt's delight upon hearing of Mrs. Bennet's news began. To say it had been a trying afternoon at Longbourn was painting the situation with a rosy brush.

Her mother had been elated – simply and loudly elated – to know that her eldest daughter was betrothed, for that was what Mr. Bingley and Jane had agreed would be the result of his discussion with her father. Added to that joyous news was the fact that her most challenging daughter had captured the eye of a man as handsome and wealthy as Mr. Darcy.

It was nearly more good fortune than Mrs. Bennet could bear. Her joy knew no bounds and bubbled forth almost incessantly.

And then, there had been Mr. Collins. Though his tone was somber, he rambled on about things as much as her mother did.

She sighed.

And like her mother, he truly was not very astute. She had not yet figured out how the man had managed to pass an exam to earn his degree. But then, she supposed, one did not need to be sensible to be intelligent, did they? Intelligence only required the individual to be interested in a particular topic and extract all they could glean from lectures and readings.

Hopefully, Mr. Collins was capable of taking whatever knowledge he possessed of Latin and Greek and the Holy Scriptures and making it flow into how he would counsel his parishioners. However, she had yet to see that he possessed such a skill.

"You look fatigued. You are not ill, are you?" Jane tucked herself into the chair next to Elizabeth.

"No, I am not ill. I am, however, tired." She glanced at Jane as she answered before returning her eyes to their mother. "Do you think she will lose her voice from all the crowing she has been doing today?"

Jane chuckled. "That is highly unlikely. You know as well as I do that she is capable of talking for hours to no ill effect."

"At least, none to her." Elizabeth closed her eyes and expelled a breath.

"You will just have to harden yourself to the fact that she is going to think of you as her best daughter for a while."

"I am not that."

"Oh, but you are. You have captured the very wealthy Mr. Darcy, who just happens to be the nephew of an earl. That is even better than I have done." Jane pressed her lips together to keep from laughing as Elizabeth rolled her eyes.

"I have not accepted him yet."

"Which is foolish."

"It is not. I have only just started to become comfortable with the idea that we could be friends." Not that she had not considered more, but it had seemed so impossible. "It is tricky leaping from there to forever as it seems you, Mother, and Mr. Darcy think I should do."

"Me, Mother, Father, Mr. Darcy, Mr. Bingley, Colonel Fitzwilliam, all of our younger sisters, and after tonight, most of the rest of Meryton." Jane fluttered her lashes. "It is only you who has not yet seen what everyone else knows must be."

"I dare say half the inhabitants of Netherfield think otherwise."

Jane chuckled. "That is not claiming support from a laudable source. Indeed, if they are your only allies and you are accepting their judgment as good, I fear you truly are ill."

Elizabeth could not help but join Jane in a laugh over that.

"Do you want to accept him?" Jane asked when they had sobered.

Elizabeth shrugged and then nodded. "I think I do, but..."

"Are you scared?"

"Yes. I truly thought choosing a husband would be easier."

"It does not have to be hard. Mr. Darcy is all that a gentleman should be, and he loves you enough to declare himself in a shop with an audience of our sisters and the store clerks."

That had been both surprising and a little bit wonderful.

"Do you think I will do him a disservice by accepting him? I know we are among the upper circle in Meryton, but he is so far above me. We are nothing compared to many in the *ton* – not to mention his relations."

Jane leaned forward and grabbed her hands. "You have the courage and mind to do whatever you determine to do. Instead of speaking your mind too freely, hold your tongue from time to time, and you will charm them all. Or, if not, then, you possess the quickest wit and sharpest tongue I know and shall make them quake at your passing."

"You are ridiculous, but I love you. Thank you." Elizabeth drew in a deep breath. She was thankful for

Jane's support, but it did little to quell the butterflies in her belly at the thought of being Mrs. Darcy. "I am not one to cower before a challenge, am I?"

"Not my Lizzy." Jane squeezed Elizabeth's hands. "Will you consider accepting him no matter how soon he offers?"

"I have promised to consider him."

"But... for how long?"

"Until my heart knows it cannot live without him." And if she were completely honest with herself and refused to indulge her trepidation about being the niece of an earl and the mistress of an estate as grand as Pemberley sounded to be, she would have to say her heart was nearly to that point already.

"Miss Bennet, Miss Elizabeth."

"Mr. Wickham," Jane greeted the gentleman who interrupted their solitude.

"I hear congratulations are in order for the both of you." He nodded his head as he sat down on the sofa across from them. "Bingley is a good chap from all I can tell," he said to Jane. "And a lucky devil as well if he has managed to convince you to marry him."

"Thank you." Jane held his gaze but said no more. While her smile may have remained in place, it was not as warm and welcoming as the one Elizabeth usually saw her sister offer to one and all.

Mr. Wickham must have felt the frostiness of his welcome, for one eyebrow cocked and his smile turned somewhat calculating. "I must say I was surprised to hear Darcy had declared himself to anyone who was not his cousin, for I had always been led to believe that he and Miss de Bourgh were destined for one another."

Elizabeth gave him an appraising look. He was handsome. There was no question about that. However, she knew what sort of a heart lay behind his pleasant façade. He was a deceiver who cared not who he hurt in the pursuit of his own gratification. "Have you ever asked him if what you believed was true or did you merely decide to believe what you wanted?"

Mr. Wickham chuckled. "I see you are sharp enough for a dour fellow like Darcy. Your beauty belies that fact. However, it is fitting. I always thought he would marry a shrew – be she pretty or otherwise."

Jane gasped.

Well, it had not taken long to expose Mr. Wickham's dislike for Mr. Darcy and all things associated with him, which now included her.

"Is Miss de Bourgh a shrew?" Elizabeth asked. "Shall I ask my cousin if it is true? He is her mother's parson, you know."

There was no way that Mr. Wickham or anyone else did not know that Mr. Collins was Lady Catherine's parson.

It was second only to his name in the way he introduced himself to anyone, and everyone, he met.

"I was not referring to Miss de Bourgh." Mr. Wickham's smile was what Elizabeth would expect a fox to wear when he was about to devour the hen to whom he was speaking. It was too bad for him that this hen would rather wear a wrap made of fox fur than attend a dinner at his house, so she returned his smile in kind.

"Oh, but you were, Mr. Wickham. For you see, you just told me that you always thought that Mr. Darcy was to marry his cousin, and then, just mere moments later, you also said you expected him to marry a shrew. Ergo, if you expected him to marry Miss de Bourgh and a shrew, that means you think Miss de Bourgh is a shrew."

Mr. Wickham's eyes narrowed.

"I say, what are you saying?"

Elizabeth's already tight smile grew tighter at Mr. Collins's question while Mr. Wickham's eyes shone with delight.

"I believe she said Miss de Bourgh is a shrew," Mr. Wickham replied. "I personally have never found her to be such."

"That is not what she said," Jane inserted. "Elizabeth, we are through trying to reason with Mr. Wickham." She stood and extended a hand to her sister. "I think our mother would be interested in what has been implied about her daughter."

"What has he implied?" Mr. Collins inquired.

"That I am a shrew, and if he was not speaking of me, then, he must have been talking about Miss de Bourgh. There are no other options. We, Miss de Bourgh and I, were the only ladies mentioned as connected to Mr. Darcy." Elizabeth sent Mr. Wickham a challenging look.

"That seems," Mr. Collins said and then paused. "It seems rather indecorous no matter who was the subject of the discourse." He gathered a handful of his jacket in each of his hands and stood taller than Elizabeth had yet seen him stand. His was of a height, which when matched with his substantial build, was rather imposing.

"It is not right that a man speaks so about the fairer sex – especially on such short acquaintance, although, I do suppose I do not know your relationship with Miss de Bourgh. Of course, I have not heard your name in all the time I have been at Rosings Park, and I am there weekly. Lady Catherine is generous and wonderfully condescending to those in her charge, and I have not witnessed her daughter being anything but as genteel as her mother – perhaps a little less prickly around the edges, but quite genteel with a delicate sort of beauty." He said this last part to Elizabeth and Jane.

"I find I must be offended on behalf of both my patron and her daughter at your words." Mr. Collins gave Wickham a severe look. It was the sort of look that Elizabeth imagined a headmaster might give to a student on the verge of receiving punishment that was harsher than a lecture.

"And then," Mr. Collins continued, "I must also be offended on the behalf of my relations. I have not known Miss Elizabeth for long. While this is true, she has presented herself as all that a young lady should be, even if she is a bit more forward about her intelligence than most." Here he gave Elizabeth a gentle smile. "I do not think that such a fault is worthy of the term shrew. I have known a shrew or two in my time, and I can tell you with absolute assurance that neither Miss Elizabeth nor Miss de Bourgh fit the description."

"Thank you," Elizabeth said when he once again gave her a gentle smile.

"Now, young man."

Elizabeth pressed her lips together to keep from giggling at the appellation Mr. Collins used for Mr. Wickham. They appeared to be very close to the same age, but, knowing that Mr. Wickham had been a childhood friend of Mr. Darcy's, she guessed Mr. Wickham was likely the eldest of the two men standing before her.

"As I see it," Mr. Collins continued, "you have two options. You may either apologize to Miss Elizabeth directly for your poor behaviour, or you may leave and never associate with my family again in any fashion. I may counsel them to be cordial in passing on the street – I would not have them cross the road to avoid you – but you will be in all other ways disassociated with them. I am positive I have the right of how Mr. Bennet would see this situation. He cares very much for his daughters and would not abide such contemptible treatment as Miss Elizabeth has received from you."

Mr. Collins lifted his chin and did a very good job of looking imperiously down his nose at Mr. Wickham, who was the shorter of the two men by at least three inches.

"What shall it be? Make your choice before we draw a crowd."

Elizabeth saw Mr. Darcy enter just then. His features took on a stony appearance when he saw Mr. Wickham standing with Elizabeth. She watched him nod and mutter his greeting before beginning to make his way to her. When she smiled at his desire to keep her from harm, she saw Mr. Wickham turn in the direction of where she was looking.

"I am sorry to have offended," he said hastily. "I shall not call you a shrew again."

"Nor anything else defamatory," Mr. Collins speared the man with another harsh look.

"Nor anything else defamatory," Mr. Wickham repeated before bowing and moving away from them.

"I do not believe he meant a word of it," Jane whispered.

Mr. Collins sighed. "That is a possibility, and not one without a great chance of being true." He looked at Elizabeth. "Are you well?"

"Yes, I am well, and I thank you for your interference."

"You are my cousin, and no matter what my father has said to me about your family or the way he behaved towards them, I am not he. I am pledged to do what is right and true, and I will not continue down the path of division and anger my father trod. Therefore, I will do what I can for you to repay the wrong that has been done by my father."

Elizabeth blinked. She had not expected that from Mr. Collins.

"We thank you," Jane said.

"Are you well?" Mr. Darcy asked as he joined them.

"Perfectly," Elizabeth replied.

"Mr. Collins has just done us a great service in extracting an apology from Mr. Wickham for Lizzy," Jane said.

"Why was an apology needed?" Concern edged a deep furrow in Mr. Darcy's brow.

"He called her a shrew."

Mr. Darcy's eyes narrowed, and his jaw clenched. That he was angry on her behalf was unmistakable. The thought spread through her soul like a warm bath did around her person when a pitcher of hot water was added to the tub.

"I am indebted to you for your help," he said to Mr. Collins.

"There is no debt to be paid." Mr. Collins was once again curled into himself. "It is what anyone would have done."

"Be that as it may, I am still grateful." Mr. Darcy said with a bow of his head.

"That is pleasure enough for me. If you will excuse me, I need to speak to your father." He bowed as he backed away and nearly collided with someone behind him.

"You truly are well?" Mr. Darcy asked.

"How could I be anything less than well when you are at my side?" She smiled impertinently, as if she was flirting with him, but she was not jesting. Her heart knew that what she said was true. It and she would be perfectly well with him.

Chapter 17

"I COULD BE AT your side forever if you would just allow it." Darcy knew it was pressing his good fortune to renew his wishes to marry her so soon after persuading her to agree to a courtship, but he wanted her to know that he desired to be her husband with all that he was.

"I know." Her head tipped as she gave him a searching look, but she said no more.

Therefore, neither did he – at least, not on that subject. So long as she knew that she was his choice, he was happy to move to other topics of conversation.

"Your mother's enthusiasm has not lessened since this afternoon."

"Nor will it for some time," Jane replied with a laugh. Her eyes only stayed on him for a moment before returning to the door of the drawing room which she had been watching.

"Bingley met Sir William in the corridor." Darcy was positive that was why Miss Bennet's eyes were watching the entry to the room. "I am sure he will join us soon."

"Is that where the colonel is as well? Is he with Mr. Bingley and Sir William?" Elizabeth asked.

Darcy shook his head. "He is in the garden with your younger sisters. He thought it best to keep an eye on them, and, having seen Mr. Wickham and heard how he spoke to you, I am glad Richard insisted on joining Miss Mary."

Elizabeth's left eyebrow arched.

"Yes, Miss Mary," Darcy said in response to the unasked question. "His words were that he wanted to make sure Miss Mary is not put upon by Mr. Collins." The man seemed harmless enough, though he was rather loquacious and fawning. Be that as it may, he was still not the gentleman whom Miss Mary wished to have paying court to her. "I am happy to hear Mr. Collins came to your defence."

"It was rather startling." Elizabeth's eyes shone with humour under raised brows. "He gave Mr. Wickham two options – either he apologized to me, or he was to be cut off from ever associating with our family again."

"And Wickham capitulated easily?" That was not how Wickham normally did things. He was the sort who would try, often successfully, to twist and turn things until he was no longer at fault of anything serious. Darcy had witnessed it both at Pemberley with his father and Wickham's father and at school with various tutors and instructors. Mr. Collins would likely be no match for such a practiced pretender.

"Surprisingly, yes, though I do not think it was simply because of Mr. Collins's demand, for you see, Mr. Wickham saw you enter, directly before he made his apology."

Ah. That did sound more like Wickham.

"He likely expected Richard to be close behind me. While I might not wish to cause a scene, my cousin is not opposed to putting on a show." He glanced toward the door that led to the small garden. "Would you care to take a walk in the garden?"

"Oh, Mr. Darcy!"

Elizabeth bit back a smile at her mother's call while Darcy tried not to grimace at the lady's interference with his plans and the high pitch of her greeting – it was very much like the first notes Georgiana had ever played on her violin.

"Mr. Darcy."

Thankfully, Mrs. Bennet's tone and volume had dropped to an easier to listen to range.

"My sister has not been properly introduced to you."

Darcy looked from Mrs. Bennet to Mrs. Philips. "We have met, and I have been shooting with her husband."

Mrs. Bennet tsked. "That is hardly enough to know one another, and since we might soon be family," she gave Elizabeth a pointed look, "you should become better acquainted."

Darcy sighed. That was hardly an argument he could refute. For that reason, he tucked away his wish to walk in the garden alone with Miss Elizabeth and capitulated. "That is true. I do hope to call you relations eventually."

Mrs. Bennet, apparently quite pleased with his response, smiled broadly at him before turning to her daughters. "Your father said he wished to speak to you and Jane. I am sure you are not needed to tell us of Mr. Darcy's connections and family. I have no doubt he is capable of doing that on his own." She made a small shooing motion with her hand in the direction of their father.

Miss Bennet immediately began crossing the room, while Elizabeth turned her eyes to Darcy. In them, he saw her concern about leaving him unattended with her mother.

"Go to your father. I will be well."

"If not, call for either my cousin or yours." Her smile was teasing, and her words made her mother huff in exasperation.

"That girl," Mrs. Bennet muttered as she shook her head. "Her tongue will be her undoing."

"I like how she speaks her mind," Darcy said. "And she seems to know where and when to do so."

Mrs. Bennet gave a short burst of laughter. "Knowing and doing are two very different things, but I should not tell you her faults. We do not wish to dissuade you from your choice."

"Nor should we, Sister," Mrs. Philips agreed. "I have always found that Lizzy keeps herself under good regulation... for the most part."

Darcy chuckled. "None of us are always successful in regulating ourselves as we should. As I am sure you know, I failed at the Michaelmas assembly. I have apologized to Miss Elizabeth and been forgiven, of course, but it is a glaring example of my not minding my tongue and my surroundings." He had been thoroughly provoked into losing his tenuous hold on himself by Bingley at the assembly, but that was not something that needed to be canvassed at present.

Mrs. Bennet placed a hand on her heart. "You are too good, Mr. Darcy. You do not need to flaunt your errors to make my Lizzy appear better than she is, and honestly," she leaned forward and dropped her voice to a whisper, as if sharing a well-guarded secret. "I knew that what you had said could not be truly what you thought."

"You did?"

Mrs. Bennet shared a smirk with her sister – it was nearly as impertinent a look as he had ever seen Elizabeth wear.

"You have eyes and seem intelligent," she replied. "Not much more is needed to know that my Lizzy is amongst the handsomest of women. She pales in comparison to her sister Jane perhaps, but she is in no way lacking. It is just that Jane's beauty is…" She shrugged and sighed. "Remarkable. She has been blessed with loveliness many times over."

"While I do not dispute that Miss Bennet is blessed with beauty, I find I must disagree with you, madame."

"Oh, surely you do not mean that Lizzy outshines Jane!" Mrs. Bennet cried.

"He must if he is to marry her." So far, in his acquaintance, Mrs. Philips seemed more perceptive than her sister.

"I am not saying either one outshines the other," Darcy inserted before the two ladies in front of him launched into a discussion of him, Miss Elizabeth, and Miss Bennet. "They are both beautiful. However, I find that I prefer Miss Elizabeth's sort of beauty to that of her sister." For laughter danced in Miss Elizabeth's eyes, care for others oozed from her soul, her wit could easily lift his spirits with a tease, and her intelligence enthralled him completely. There was not another like her. She was, to him, perfection.

The lady who owned his heart and captured his imagination chose that exact moment as he glanced her way to smile at him from across the room. Then, she gave her father a peck on the cheek and pointed surreptitiously toward the door to the garden.

Darcy gave a small nod of his head.

That action caught the attention of Mrs. Philips and Mrs. Bennet who turned to see Miss Elizabeth moving toward the door.

"Oh, you cannot go with her until we know more about you!" Mrs. Bennet cried.

Yes, that was why he was still standing in the drawing room rather than out in the garden. "Then, what would you like to know?" Perhaps a more direct approach would get him to where he wanted to be more quickly.

Mrs. Philips chuckled. "He seems in a hurry, Sister."

"I cannot blame him. He has not yet convinced her to marry him you know."

"Oh, yes, I know," Mrs. Philips agreed with alacrity and a shake of her head, as if Miss Elizabeth's not having already accepted Darcy was the strangest thing she had ever heard.

"As do I," Darcy inserted, causing both ladies to giggle. "What can I tell you about myself that you do not already know? I am certain you have learned of my wealth and estate already. I cannot fathom that Mr. Collins has not already told you that my aunt, Lady Catherine de Bourgh, is his patroness and that she has one daughter, my cousin Anne – who, by the by, I am not betrothed to, nor have I ever been betrothed to her. However, my aunt would like for me to marry her daughter and has circulated that desire for years."

Mrs. Bennet gasped. "Will your aunt hate my Lizzy?"

That was a real concern, but not one that would dissuade Darcy from his purpose.

"She may for a while, but I will not tolerate anyone treating your daughter poorly whether they are family, friends, or strangers."

"You are too good." Mrs. Bennet's hand was, once again, on her heart and what looked to be tears glistened in her eyes. "Lizzy is fortunate to have you." Her brow furrowed. "Well, she will be once she comes to her senses, that is." She shook her head and sighed as if Miss Elizabeth not reaching the desired end was a real concern to her.

After the few moments Darcy had spent with Miss Elizabeth in this drawing room this evening, he was less concerned and more confident about her acceptance than he had been all day.

"Thank you for your kind words, but I am only doing what is right by the one I love."

This elicited a sigh from both ladies.

"You have met my cousin Colonel Fitzwilliam. He has an older brother, the Viscount, and a younger brother, Robert, who is yet in school. His parents are the Earl and Countess of Matlock. I do believe those are all my relations and connections of note. However, I also have two uncles and an aunt who were siblings of my father. They all have various properties in the north, which are smaller than Pemberley – my father was the heir -- and they also all have children who I call cousins."

"The colonel has a younger brother in school?" There was a decided note of interest in Mrs. Bennet's tone as she asked the question. "What is he studying?"

"Law."

"A noble profession," Mrs. Philips said with a smile.

"And he is unmarried?" Mrs. Bennet queried.

Darcy chuckled. "Yes, both he and Richard have yet to please their mother by taking a wife. Not that my aunt would want her youngest to marry until he is established."

"That does make sense." Mrs. Bennet's brow furrowed as if she were reasoning something out. "The colonel seems to be paying particular attention to my Mary."

"He does."

"Do you think he is merely being friendly?" she asked the question in a low whisper as her eyes darted left and right to see if anyone was close enough to hear her.

"That is what I would assume until told otherwise."

Mrs. Bennet's brow was once again furrowed. "I suppose that is the best, but it would not hurt to encourage him otherwise, would it?"

"I try not to meddle in affairs of the heart, so my advice would be to let things unfold as they are supposed to do."

This was met with a serious look and a nod of the lady's head. "I suppose I shall content myself with encouraging a friendship. Some of the best marriages begin that way, or so I have been told."

"Indeed, they do. That is how my husband and I began. Fanny and Thomas were more like Jane and Mr. Bingley – instantly in love upon first meeting."

"And still that way now." The matriarch of the Bennet family turned to look at her husband who nodded and winked in reply to her small wave.

Darcy had not thought that there was much love between the Miss Elizabeth's parents, but it seemed as if he were wrong on that account. Their love was not easily discernable, but if he were to believe the exchange he had just witnessed and Mrs. Bennet's words, their marriage was founded on love.

She smiled at Darcy when she turned back towards him. "Go to Lizzy. We can learn more about you later. I would not wish to keep you from the object of your affection."

"That is kind of you." Darcy said as his attention was captured by Wickham just entering the garden. "And I will do as you say in a moment, but I have just remembered that there is one more thing you need to know about me."

"I am sure you can tell me later."

"No, this really cannot wait. Have you met Mr. Wickham?"

"Oh, yes! He is a handsome and charming fellow," Mrs. Philips replied while her sister nodded her agreement.

"He and I used to be friends."

"Used to be?" Mrs. Philips repeated.

Darcy nodded. "His father was my father's steward and friend, which often brought us together, and over time a friendship of sorts established itself – it was never a close friendship, but it was a friendship nonetheless. When my father died, Mr. Wickham, who was his godson, was left a living in his will and a sum of one thousand pounds. However," he said quickly as he took note of Mrs. Bennet's excited expression, "he did not wish to take orders, and we settled on three thousand pounds as his inheritance in lieu of the living. As you have noticed, he has now joined himself to the militia. That is not because he has some sense of duty that must be fulfilled. It is because he has spent his inheritance and is in need of funds."

"Surely not!" Mrs. Bennet looked horrified.

"It is the truth. He spent it all in dissipated living, and then, about a year ago, he came to me to claim the living he had previously refused. I denied him his request, for it is my opinion that he is not fit for the church, and he had already been paid the sum I mentioned in place of the living. Needless to say, he does not like me, and, frankly, I do not like what he has become.

"As I said, we were once friends, but he has contrived to harm me in a most grievous way because of his anger at my refusal to give him that living. Do not trust him – especially with your daughters. I cannot say more than that, but please, take care. Young unmarried ladies are never truly safe in his presence, for he is a charmer. The reason, however, that this information could not wait until later to be shared is that I fear his dislike for me may extend to those who are dear to me. In light of that, your care should be even greater."

Mrs. Bennet was fanning herself ferociously as Darcy concluded.

"I hope I have not overset you too much, but I felt you should know."

"Oh, we are grateful to you," Mrs. Philips said. "Are we not, Sister?"

"Most assuredly."

"Now, if you will excuse me, I would very much like to take your suggestion and join your daughter in the garden before we eat." And he also wanted to make sure that Wickham was not importuning Miss Elizabeth or her sisters.

Chapter 18

THE EVENING WAS COOL, but not unbearably so. Despite that, Elizabeth pulled her wrap more snuggly around herself to ward off the chill as she walked down the central path in her aunt and uncle's garden. While it was not a large garden, it was pretty, even now when it was devoid of the colourful blossoms that painted it with cheer during the spring and summer.

Torches, which were a necessity if one wanted to enjoy a garden in the evening at this time of year since the shadows of night insisted upon creeping in earlier and earlier each day, cast pools of light on the central path as well as the several shorter paths that branched out from it. Her aunt, just like her mother, had a keen eye for garden design.

Reaching the center of the garden, Elizabeth turned and looked for her three younger sisters. It did not take long to spot two of them, Lydia and Kitty, chatting with Maria Lucas near the front of the garden on the side where the gate faced the road. Before heading in their direction, however, she turned again, intent upon finding Mary.

Ah! There she was, walking on Colonel Fitzwilliam's arm. Elizabeth pulled the corner of her bottom lip between her teeth as she watched them for a moment. The colonel's head dipped toward her sister's as he spoke to her, and she hoped that Mary's heart was not being put in danger by the colonel. There was nothing she could do beyond worry, however. Therefore, she would leave Mary to the colonel's care for now.

Before Mr. Darcy joined her, she did want to at least check on her youngest sisters and inquire after her particular friend, Charlotte Lucas, Maria's older sister. To that end, she turned toward the front of the garden and took the path to her left.

"Good evening, Maria," she said as she approached the trio of young ladies.

"Good evening, Lizzy."

Maria was a pleasant young lady who was just as excitable as Lydia and Kitty but with a sweeter and quieter disposition. Or so it seemed to someone who did not have to live under the same roof with her. Charlotte might disagree with Elizabeth on her assessment.

"I have not seen Charlotte."

Maria's expression turned sad. "She is not well."

"I hope it is nothing serious."

Maria shook her head. "It is just a sore throat and a cough, but Mama would not hear of her leaving the house."

"That is unfortunate. I had hoped to see her tonight. You will give her my love when you go home, will you not?"

"Along with your news," Maria said. "I cannot wait to share that! It is rather exciting to hear that both you and your sister are to marry such handsome and wealthy men."

"I am not betrothed." Why did everyone immediately jump to that conclusion? It was not as if every courtship ended in marriage. Many did, but not all.

"But you will be," Maria replied. "Mr. Darcy is perfection. Surely, you would not be able to refuse him. Kitty and Lydia say he adores you." She sighed wistfully.

"I do not know if I would say he adores me." Elizabeth laughed lightly, though the idea was not an unwelcome one nor one that she necessarily thought of as false.

"That is only because you are too stubborn to admit the truth." Lydia lifted her chin and peered down her nose at Elizabeth. "It is plain enough for everyone else to see."

"You only see it because he spoke to Papa."

"He said he adored you in the milliner's shop," Kitty said.

"He did not –"

Lydia did not let Elizabeth finish her protest. "And I had suspected it when we were at Netherfield, although I did not think you would have him, but then, you seemed agreeable in the milliner's shop."

"You suspected nothing of the sort at Netherfield!" Elizabeth had barely suspected it herself at that time.

"She most certainly did!" Kitty cried. "In the carriage, on the way home, Lydia told me that she thought Mr. Darcy no longer found you only tolerable, for why else would he be so welcoming of Mama and us?"

"Because he is a proper gentleman and knows how to be polite." And because they had become friends that morning. That was all she had thought it was – friendship. She had had no inkling that he possessed any feeling for her beyond camaraderie at the time.

Lydia shook her head. "He was not polite at the assembly, so I doubt he would have been so welcoming if he had not changed his opinion of you." She looked at Maria. "His was a faulty opinion anyway. Lizzy is not me or Jane, but she is far prettier than merely tolerable. Miss King is merely tolerable, and Lizzy is no Miss King."

"Lydia, that is not kind," Elizabeth scolded.

"But it is true," Lydia retorted.

"True or not, it should not be said." Elizabeth shifted her attention to Maria. There was no way to win this argument about Mr. Darcy when Lydia already had her mind set so firmly on things being as she saw them. It would be best to move on. "Do tell Charlotte I missed her."

Having received Maria's assurance that her message would be delivered to Charlotte, Elizabeth took herself in the direction of the kitchen garden. There was a bench near there where she could sit and watch the door for Mr. Darcy.

She would not admit it to her sisters for all the ribbons and lace in the world, but she was almost certain that Mr. Darcy did adore her, and she hoped he did. Though she could admit such things to herself, it was not something she felt comfortable embracing so fully that she would admit to it or share it with one and all.

Presently, she only tentatively held it in her heart that it was true, but, as she took her seat to watch the door for the gentleman of her contemplations, she had to acknowledge, that it would take very little for *her* to adore *him* utterly and irreversibly.

He was handsome and rich, that was true. However, for her, those were only pleasant extras. His character shone like finely polished brass and seemed as unbreakable as the strongest bar of iron. And his heart... She sighed. His heart was tender. He loved his sister dearly and extended himself for his friends – even when he did not want to be at an assembly or away from his sister. He truly was among the best of men. Why was she dithering about whether to allow her heart to love him as it wished or not? Perhaps everyone else had the right of it. She should be betrothed to him. The thought sent a skitter of excited nerves racing in her belly and brought a smile to her lips. Perhaps she would tell him when he joined her.

"He has said something to them about me."

Mr. Wickham's words interrupted Elizabeth's thoughts. She turned her head slightly to see to whom he was talking. He and Captain Denny stood one path over from the one that took a person to this bench. She scooted down the bench some to be more fully hidden in the shadows there.

"You cannot know that for certain," Captain Denny said.

"There is no other reason why Miss Elizabeth was so cold to me, and her sisters – the youngest ones – were uncharacteristically unwelcoming earlier."

"I would not fret too much over it, Wickham. There are other young ladies in Meryton. The Bennets are not the only ones, and as you have told me, you, unlike me, need a lady with a fortune. They do not have that."

"But what Miss Lydia lacks in fortune, she makes up for in other areas."

Both Mr. Wickham and Captain Denny chuckled at that, while indignation at the implication of their words bubbled up inside Elizabeth and wished to burst forth in a sharp reprimand. However, she held her tongue, but later, she would make sure to mention Captain Denny's participation in such a conversation to her father. He was already ill-disposed to think well of Wickham or any of his associates after hearing what Mr. Collins had shared with him, and what Jane and Elizabeth had confirmed, about their conversation with Mr. Wickham in the drawing room.

"I could already have a lady and a fortune if it were not for *him*." Mr. Wickham's tone was laced with disgust.

"You could have the lady without her fortune if you truly cared for her as you claimed to me you did."

That comment pulled Mr. Denny partially out of the pit into which Elizabeth had thrown his character at his laughing about what Lydia possessed other than a fortune.

"No, I could not. My heart in the matter had very little to do with my choice in walking away as I did. I could not provide for her or myself without her fortune."

Elizabeth blinked. Had Mr. Wickham actually cared about Miss Darcy? No, surely not. He was a rogue – both Mr. Darcy and the colonel said he was. He had schemed to visit Miss Darcy secretly.

"You could likely do better financially if your pocketbook were not so easily lightened. There is much good that can come from refraining from pleasure on occasion."

Wickham's chuckle lacked any mirth. "You sound like my father. I do not know how many times he said something like that to either me or my mother."

"It sounds as if your father was wise."

"Or just lacking a sense of adventure and good taste."

"I say wise," Captain Denny protested.

"Say what you will. It does not make you right."

Nor did it make him wrong!

There was only a grunt of displeasure from Captain Denny in reply to Mr. Wickham's comment.

"I ought to…" Mr. Wickham's words fell away, and Elizabeth peeked over her shoulder at him. He was pacing in front of Denny with his hand on his chin as if he were thinking.

"I have it," he cried as he came to a stop in front of Captain Denny. "He does not want news of his sister's near ruin to spread. I dare say he'd be willing to pay for it."

"You would use the lady you claim to have loved to gain a few coins?"

That settled it. Wickham was a rogue and had not truly cared for Miss Darcy.

"A few coins? Darcy has more than a few coins, and I am willing to bet that his sister is worth a great number of coins to him."

"You rarely win a wager," Captain Denny grumbled, "which is why you have so few coins yourself."

"I cannot lose."

"And you always say that! However, history proves it is not true. Where is the money you had after old Mr. Darcy died? Hmmm?"

"That was merely a streak of bad luck."

"An expensive one," Captain Denny grumbled.

"I gained you as a friend during that time, so not all was lost."

There was a patronizing chuckle that met the comment. "And I am the only friend you had then who is still willing to be your friend now, and as your friend, let me remind you that you are not just betting against Darcy but also his cousin."

"That is more concerning," Mr. Wickham agreed.

Elizabeth tapped her leg nervously. Surely, her mother would be done with Mr. Darcy soon, and he would appear and stop Mr. Wickham from plotting before the man landed on an idea that might actually work.

Mr. Wickham snapped his fingers.

"What is it?" Denny asked.

"Brilliance," Mr. Wickham replied. "Utter brilliance. Come along and witness it if you wish."

"Where are you going, and what are you doing?"

"You are too cautious."

"I like to keep my money and my life."

Elizabeth looked and saw the two men moving toward the front of the garden.

"Then keep your voice down. This garden is not large, and the colonel is not hard of hearing."

Elizabeth rose from her place and began moving toward the center of the garden so she could still hear them without appearing to follow them.

"What is your plan?" Denny pressed.

"To woo a fortune-less lass and become Darcy's brother."

"She was not welcoming earlier."

"She does not have to be welcoming to end up my bride."

"No," Denny said. "Forster will not be pleased if you compromise her. He has told us that very specifically, and you do not know how he is when angry."

Elizabeth did not wait to hear more. She gathered a bit of her skirt in each hand and, lifting her hem, walked through the garden beds from the path she was on to the one traversed by Captain Denny and Mr. Wickham.

"Do not do it!" she cried as she shook out her skirt and stamped her feet to remove any dirt that clung to her slippers.

Both men stopped and turned toward her.

"I will not allow it." There was no way Elizabeth was going to let her sisters be in harm's way if it were in her power to prevent it.

"I do not see how you can prevent me from doing what I want." Mr. Wickham crossed his arms and sneered at her.

"Wickham," Captain Denny growled.

"She cannot always be watching her sister, nor can she prevent her sister from falling for my charm."

"You will not be allowed to call on her. My father was not pleased to hear what you called me earlier."

Captain Denny took a step away from Mr. Wickham. "What did he call you?"

"A shrew."

"Indeed?" Captain Denny said.

"She provoked me."

"I did," Elizabeth agreed.

"Did you tell your sisters to not speak to me?" Mr. Wickham asked.

Elizabeth shook her head. "That was Colonel Fitzwilliam."

"Darcy and his cousin!" Mr. Wickham spat on the ground. "I knew it was one of them. They continually treat me ill – withholding my inheritance, denying me my heart. I have had enough of it."

"Nothing was denied you," Elizabeth said. "And I dare say your heart was never involved with the lady you importuned."

Mr. Wickham's head tipped to one side as his left eyebrow arched. "Well, well, well, Darcy is telling tales, is he? I dare say he must be confident in securing you as his wife." Even in the less-than-ideal light of the torches, Elizabeth could see his eyes sweep up and down her person. "If he is telling tales, then I do not see why I cannot as well."

"The colonel," Captain Denny whispered.

"Who will know if it was me or Darcy's beloved who shared the story?"

"I would never!"

"Perhaps it was overheard."

Elizabeth shook her head.

"Either you are the source of rumors, or I charm myself into Darcy family through your sister." He turned toward where Lydia and Kitty were still talking to Maria. "Shall it be Miss Lydia or Miss Kitty?" He cast a look over his shoulder at Elizabeth.

"I will have no part of this," Captain Denny said.

"You will tell no one, for you do not wish Forster to find out what I know about you and the lady he has been courting."

"It was before he met her."

"Was it?"

"Wickham." The name rumbled from Captain Denny.

"Is it just his lack of money or his propensity to use people for his own purposes that has found him so lacking in friends?" Elizabeth asked the captain.

"Apparently, both," Captain Denny replied.

"I am still waiting for your decision, Miss Elizabeth. Which sister shall bring me what I want? Miss Lydia, Miss Kitty, or Darcy's?"

Elizabeth's heart raced. She could not choose any of the sisters listed. She would not. There had to be something else that would appease Mr. Wickham. "What exactly do you seek? Money or to harm Mr. Darcy? Which is most important?"

He turned toward her as a satisfied smile turned his lips upward. To Elizabeth it was the very image of how she had always pictured the devil to look when the parson spoke about him in sermons.

"I suppose if I had to choose..." He paused. "Money is nice. Darcy's money is better."

"Why? Why is Mr. Darcy's money better?"

Mr. Wickham chuckled. "Because then, I would have money, and Darcy would have pain."

"Then, let me give you what you wish." Elizabeth drew a steadying breath and willed the pain in her heart to stay where it was and not keep her from doing what she knew she needed to do to keep both her sisters and Mr. Darcy's sister safe. "If you wish to cause Mr. Darcy pain, I can provide that."

She swallowed as tears gathered. "I will end my courtship with him and send him away when he comes to call, but in exchange you will never tell another soul about his sister, nor will you ever call on or even speak to one of my sisters again."

Mr. Wickham studied her for a moment before nodding. "I think that might work. However, if you renege on our agreement, *his* sister will be the first to feel the sting."

Elizabeth put out her hand. It only trembled a little. "Then, we have an understanding."

Chapter 19

Darcy stepped into the garden later than he had expected to do because his hasty escape to meet Elizabeth had, thanks to Sir William, been thwarted by an introduction to, followed by a brief discussion with, Colonel Forster. While the meeting had delayed Darcy, it had also seemed an excellent idea to become acquainted with the man in charge of Wickham.

Forster, a gentleman only a few years Darcy's senior, seemed to be an upstanding sort of fellow who accepted very little foolishness from his men. The lady on his arm, however, had seemed less grounded and more flighty.

Apparently, Miss Gilbert, the colonel's betrothed, was one of Miss Lydia's intimate friends. Darcy could see why the two were friends as they did seem to share some traits – such as a fondness for ribbons and lace, if Miss Gilbert's dress was any indication, for it had been a well-festooned concoction.

Of course, the future Mrs. Forster's similarities to Miss Lydia held no bearing on how Wickham would be handled in the militia. On that front, Darcy was certain that the colonel was the sort of man who would hold Wickham to a standard of behaviour that Wickham did not naturally possess.

Therefore, Darcy was only mildly frustrated with his late arrival in the garden, for the information gathered was the sort to put his mind at ease as far as it could be put at ease when Wickham was the subject.

Now, with his duty to all others safely behind him, he had only to find Miss Elizabeth and spend a few minutes walking with her before having to sit at supper and converse with his neighbours. He had promised himself and Mrs. Hurst that he was going to improve his image in the community – to right his wrongs – and he intended to make a valiant attempt at keeping that promise tonight.

Darcy's eyes scanned the paths from right to left, searching for the lady who held his heart. It still amazed him that he had fallen in love so quickly and without being completely aware of it until it had happened.

Richard and Miss Mary were at the top of the garden, making their way to the center. On the path to Richard's left, it appeared Bingley had been successful in securing a stroll in the evening air with Miss Bennet.

Darcy's observation of his surroundings came forward and halted. His breath caught at the sight upon which his gaze had landed. Was that Miss Elizabeth with Wickham? And why was Wickham's companion flapping a hand behind his hat as if he were trying to draw attention and yet not be seen?

Darcy did not wait to ponder the *why's* and *what's* of the situation. Instead, he began making his way toward Miss Elizabeth with long, rapid strides, keeping Elizabeth in his view as he did.

Wait! His steps faltered. What was she doing? Why was she extending her hand to that scoundrel, and why in the name of everything good was that ne'er-do-well kissing Elizabeth's hand?

Darcy began to run.

"I will not allow you to do this, Miss Elizabeth." Wickham's friend – Captain Denny, if Darcy were remembering correctly – extended his arm so that his wave was higher and more exaggerated.

"Remember what I know," Wickham barked as he dropped Elizabeth's hand and lunged toward his friend.

"I will tell Forster I kissed his lady to win a bet myself. I would rather risk the skin on my back than watch you harm another lady. The Bennets have been all that is kind and welcoming to me. I cannot in good conscience let Miss Elizabeth do what she is so nobly attempting to do."

"What is she attempting to do?" Darcy breathed hard and fast as he came to where Captain Denny, Wickham, and his Elizabeth stood. He looked to Elizabeth for an answer, but she only pressed her lips together and shook her head as a tear slipped down her cheek.

"What have you done to her?" Darcy growled as he grabbed Wickham by the arm.

Wickham tried, unsuccessfully, to extract his arm from Darcy's grip. "I have done nothing, nor do I know what Denny is babbling on about."

Darcy glanced at Denny who advanced a step on Wickham.

"I have stood by you and believed your lies about this or that misbehaviour being the last time or a sad misfortune or something that you had not contemplated thoroughly." Denny's tone was calm but heated. "I have trusted you to make the changes you said you would. It is why you have your position in the militia. Do you even remember what you promised me to get it?"

"It seems my friend has stumbled and hit his head, for I am certain he speaks nonsense," Wickham said.

"You expect me to believe you?" Darcy twisted Wickham's arm behind his back and pressed against him so that he could speak close to Wickham's ear. "I let you go far too easily the last time. I will not make the same mistake twice. Now tell me what you have done to Miss Elizabeth."

"He has extracted an agreement after threatening her sisters and yours." Denny stood close to Wickham with arms folded across his chest.

"Denny." There was a threatening tone to Wickham's grumble. "One friend does not betray another."

Denny laughed bitterly. "That is rich coming from you and holds no bearing on our present circumstances, for, as of this moment, we are no longer friends."

His eyes returned to Darcy. "Miss Elizabeth is to turn you away in exchange for both Wickham's staying clear of her sisters and not forcing any of them to become his wife and for his keeping his knowledge of what happened at Ramsgate from being spread throughout Hertfordshire and beyond."

Darcy turned his head to look at Elizabeth. "Is this true?"

Tears fell steadily down her cheeks as she nodded. "It was the only way I could think of to keep them all safe." Her shoulders lifted and lowered in a small shrug, which, along with her tears, told him that she had not wished to make the agreement.

Darcy gave Wickham a shove towards Denny. "Do with him what you will. If Forster has any questions, send him to me and I will vouch for you." Releasing Wickham's arm, Darcy turned to Elizabeth and pulled her into his arms.

"I am sorry," she said. "I did not know another way."

"Thank you," he whispered against her hair.

"Uh, Darcy?" Bingley said as he and the colonel joined them. "What are you doing?"

"Remove that blackguard from this garden," Darcy said to his cousin.

"It would be my pleasure. If you will excuse me for a moment, Miss Mary." Richard stepped away from her.

"I can remove myself," Wickham said hastily.

"Oh, but I do not think so." Denny grabbed Wickham's left arm. "May I assist you in throwing out the refuse, Colonel?"

Richard sent a questioning look to Darcy, who nodded. Captain Denny may have kept questionable company up until now, but there was no denying the great service he had done for Elizabeth.

"What has happened?" Miss Mary asked.

Darcy dropped a kiss on Elizabeth's hair. Could he love her more than he did at this moment? He was not sure he could. "Your sister has put herself and her heart in the way of danger to save your sisters and mine from any of Mr. Wickham's treacherous schemes."

"How so?" Bingley asked. "And we are drawing the notice of a many. You may wish to unhand Miss Elizabeth."

Reluctantly, Darcy released Elizabeth from his embrace and fished his handkerchief from his pocket for her to dry her tears.

"My understanding is that Miss Elizabeth heard Wickham plotting to either secure one of her sisters as his wife or to share details he knows about my sister as gossip to discredit her. I am not, however, entirely sure why he was plotting such things."

"He wanted to harm you and get your money," Elizabeth said as she dried her eyes and sniffled. "Harming you seemed to be foremost in his mind." She looked down at the handkerchief she gripped tightly in her hands. "That is why I told him I would send you away. I knew it would hurt you, and the idea of causing you pain seemed to delight him." She shook her head. "I did not want to send you away, but I could think of nothing else I could do to save our sisters. I could not let what he planned happen to them... or to you." She lifted tear-filled eyes to Darcy. "Can you forgive me for what surely looks like a betrayal?"

Darcy took her hands in his. "You have betrayed no one. There is nothing to forgive."

"But I was going to send you away. I was not just telling Mr. Wickham one thing and planning to do another. I would have refused to allow you to call on me."

"But you would not have done so happily, would you have?"

"No." A few tears slid down her cheek as if to emphasize her point. "But how can you trust me if I am willing to give you up..." her words faded away into a shrug.

"You have not betrayed my trust. If anything, you have confirmed that I was right to trust you with my heart. You were not just thinking of the harm that Wickham would do to our sisters, were you?" She had said she could not allow it to happen to him – not just her sisters or his. "You knew that Wickham's plans were designed to do more harm to me than to either my sister or yours, did you not?"

She shrugged again but then, nodded. "I could not let you be tied to such a man, nor could I willingly let your heart be shattered when your sister's present and future happiness would be tainted by vicious rumours."

There seemed to be a rather sizable crowd standing around them now. Darcy could see Miss Lydia and Miss Kitty to his left, and he heard shuffling behind him. Bingley, Miss Bennet, and Miss Mary were still in front of him but behind Elizabeth.

He was not one to speak openly about his feelings to one and all, and he suspected Miss Elizabeth was not such a person either. However, he needed to know her reason for doing as she had done, and he hoped it was because of what he suspected. If it was, he was about to make a very public offer of marriage to the lady he loved.

"Why did you care if my heart was injured?" he asked his question quietly, gently.

Elizabeth closed her eyes and drew a breath. Then, opening her eyes, she peeked around them before leaning forward and whispering, "I love you."

Darcy wanted to wrap her once again in his arms at such wonderful words, but he refrained.

"Enough to now accept my offer of marriage?" He held her eyes with his and saw the small smile that lifted her cheeks and began to shine in her lovely eyes. "You are the lady of whom my father wrote, but beyond that, you are the lady whom I love very dearly and know, with all that is within me, is best suited to me to be my bride, the mistress of my homes, the mother of my children, and my companion for as long as God grants me life. Do you love me enough to marry me?"

The light in her eyes was nearly dancing as she nodded. "I do. I truly, truly do."

Next to him, Miss Lydia gasped and clapped her hands, but the agreement was not yet made. So far, Darcy had only discovered that Miss Elizabeth was willing to entertain an offer.

"Will you marry me?"

She laughed lightly. "Yes, I will happily marry you."

"It appears," Bingley said in a teasing tone, "that the madness has spread."

This comment, referring to her first response to Darcy's presenting the idea of marriage to her, drew a small laugh from Elizabeth. "Indeed, it appears it has." Her eyes did not leave Darcy's. "But it is a happy madness."

"I am delighted to hear it," Bingley continued. "Allow me to be the first to wish you joy." He inserted himself between Darcy and Elizabeth to offer his hand first to Elizabeth and then, to Darcy.

Darcy arched a brow at the interference. He had no wish to let go of Elizabeth's hand. Indeed, he wanted to kiss her

– and not just on her knuckles, but properly, as is only natural for a man violently in love.

"Her father is steps from us," Bingley whispered. "As are half, if not all, of the invited guests. Kiss her later." He gave Darcy a pointed look.

Ah, that was a good suggestion.

"What is happening?" He heard Mrs. Bennet's voice above the others.

Darcy smiled and, taking his Elizabeth's hand, turned toward his future mother-in-law, ready to proclaim his good news in securing her promise to marry him. However, he was not quick enough.

"Lizzy is going to marry Mr. Darcy, Mama!" Lydia cried. "She is not so lacking in sense as you feared."

Mr. Bennet chuckled as he pushed his way to where Darcy was. "I did not think you would succeed in your quest so quickly, though I did know you would succeed." He looked at Elizabeth. "You are happy?" There was a question in his voice and expression as he studied her face.

She nodded. "I know I do not look it, but I am."

"I am surprised you have changed your mind as rapidly as you did," her father pressed. "Is there a reason?"

"Mr. Wickham," Lydia answered.

Her father turned to his youngest daughter with a startled expression. "Mr. Wickham?" he repeated, turning to look at the people gathered, as if he were searching for the man.

"He is not here," Lydia continued. "The colonel and Captain Denny threw him out, and good riddance, I say."

Darcy saw Mr. Bennet's brow furrow.

"Threw him out?" Mrs. Bennet cried. "Threw him out? I suppose I knew he was not worthy of any of my daughters, but threw him out?"

"He is not fit company, Mama. He just is not." Lydia lifted her chin. "A lady who is any sort of lady at all does not even contemplate flirting with a scoundrel like him." She sighed. "Even is he is a handsome scoundrel." Here, she inserted another sigh. "I would not want him nor would Kitty."

Lydia turned to Elizabeth and smiled. "Thank you," she said softly.

"Indeed," Kitty muttered.

Mr. Bennet's brow was still furrowed.

"Perhaps over dinner, I can share the reason for the removal of Wickham from our society," Darcy offered. "Would that be agreeable?"

"Only if you do it loudly enough for us all to hear," Mrs. Bennet said.

"It would save the gossips some trouble," Mr. Bennet agreed.

Darcy laughed. "Very well, I shall tell what I can so that all can hear just as long as Miss Elizabeth and Captain Denny do not mind."

"They will know whether you tell it or not," Elizabeth assured him. "Someone will surely tell Mama." She winked at her youngest sister who smiled and ducked her head.

"And I am not opposed to your relation of the incident." Captain Denny had rejoined them along with the colonel.

"Then, it is settled," Mrs. Philips cried. "This shall be a dinner to be remembered for some time. It is so good to have Mr. Darcy as part of our group, is it not?" She made a shooing motion towards the house. "But we do not wish for our meal to grow cold."

As the crowd began to disperse, Mr. Bennet called to his sister-in-law, and having gained her attention, said, "I think it is best if we older folks get settled while the younger set takes one more turn of the garden."

A smile graced Mrs. Philips's face as Mr. Bennet tipped his head toward Darcy.

"I do believe you have the right of it, but I had hoped Lydia would help me with the arrangement of everyone. She is very good at deciding conversation partners."

"Oh, I am," Miss Lydia cried in delight. "We do not mind going in first, do we Kitty and Maria?"

"No, not at all," the two other young ladies said.

Darcy shook his head. He was not just marrying a lady who was well-versed in gently guiding others to do as they wished them to do. He was marrying into a family that seemed to have a good supply of such ladies... and gentlemen, he added as Mr. Bennet gave him a wink and his daughter's hand a pat before leaving them alone.

"We will walk ahead of you," Bingley said as he gave a nod of his head toward the back of the garden to Richard.

Then, with everyone else moved away from them, Darcy lifted Elizabeth's hand to his lips. "We have very cleverly been left alone."

"Indeed, we have."

"May I kiss you?"

Her smile was welcoming. "I do think it is required to seal our agreement, is it not?"

He chuckled. "I believe you have the right of it." And without further delay, he pulled her to him and kissed her.

Chapter 20

Raindrops splattered against the window for a fourth day in a row as Darcy opened his book and then closed it again.

"Is your book lacking in interest?" There was a hopeful note to Mrs. Hurst's question.

"I just grow tired of reading," Darcy admitted. He glanced at Richard who was lounging near the window with his eyes closed. Hurst was not far away doing the same thing. Perhaps Darcy should follow their example to avoid having to converse with either of Bingley's sisters.

"Caroline could play for us," Mrs. Hurst suggested.

"She has no need to display her talents, Louisa. Darcy is betrothed to be married," Bingley said from where he sat at the desk sketching. The man could not write a letter legibly enough to be easily deciphered, but he was far more than merely adequate when it came to drawing. It was just part and parcel of what made up the complexity of his friend.

"But he is bored," Mrs. Hurst protested.

"Do you think the roads are completely impassable?" Darcy asked, ignoring Mrs. Hurst's comment about his need for entertainment.

Richard popped open an eye. "It is quite likely a carriage would get stuck."

"But a horse?" Darcy asked hopefully. He would do anything to be able to get out of the house and perhaps be allowed to see Elizabeth.

"You would be soaked before you got to Longbourn," Bingley said. "I stood outside for twenty minutes this morning to test that very fact."

"Did you try two coats?" Hurst asked without opening his eyes.

"Are you not sleeping?" Mrs. Hurst asked her husband.

"As you can hear," he replied. "Have you done all that needs doing to help ensure your sister looks the part of a grand hostess at Charles's ball?"

"There are only so many times we can go over the menu and check on the cleaning."

"And Cook has barred them from the kitchen," Bingley added.

"It is too bad we do not have a greenhouse, is it not, Caroline? Then, we could be selecting and arranging flowers." She sighed dramatically.

Miss Bingley said nothing, which was what she had been saying a lot of since the dinner at the Philips's house. She was not pleased with Darcy's betrothal, but she seemed unwilling to press the issue in his presence – unlike her sister.

"Hurst could set up a card table," Mrs. Hurst suggested.

"I do not want to play cards." Richard rose from his repose. "I am going outside. The rain does not sound as heavy now as it did earlier." He looked at Darcy. "Will you join me?"

Darcy did not need to be asked twice.

"But you might become ill!" Mrs. Hurst cried. "And then, what will become of our ball?"

"We can sleep while you dance," Richard answered.

"And who will dance with Miss Elizabeth if Mr. Darcy sleeps through the ball?" Caroline asked. "It would be a shame to see her left standing... again." Her eyes were still fixed on the needlework she was doing, but, from where Darcy was standing, he could still see the sly smile she wore.

"We will not become ill," Darcy assured her, "for we will make sure we are warm and dry as soon as we return."

"And I have been wet for days and not fallen ill, so you have nothing to fear on my account," Richard added as he followed Darcy from the room. "Do you think we could make it to Longbourn before becoming too wet?" he whispered as they walked down the hall to the staircase.

"Bingley seems to think we cannot." Darcy shot his cousin a curious look. "I know why I am anxious to go to

Longbourn, but I do not know why you are – except, of course, that you wish to be free from Mrs. Hurst."

Richard chuckled. "That alone would be a good enough reason, but no, it is not my true reason." He began climbing the stairs, taking two at a time and causing Darcy to hurry to keep up with him.

"Is it Miss Mary?" Darcy asked as they gained the landing.

During their walk in the garden at the Philips's house, Richard had successfully convinced Miss Mary to allow him to stand as a buffer between her and Mr. Collins, and Darcy had to admit that the man was putting on a stage-worthy performance in playing the part of a potential suitor. He was doing so well that Mrs. Bennet was certain her most serious daughter might not be as suited to the life of a parson's wife as she was to life as the wife of a colonel, and Elizabeth was still worried about the potential harm his cousin might do to her sister's heart.

Richard nodded. "How can I keep her from Mr. Collins's advances when I am here? I would rather be doing my duty than hiding from it." His brow furrowed deeply as he scowled. "When we were at Longbourn two days ago, did you hear her commending him on his demand that Wickham apologize to Miss Elizabeth?"

Darcy shook his head. He had paid little attention to any conversation, save the one he had had with Elizabeth.

Richard blew out a breath. "It was as if the man had rid the world of Old Boney!"

Was that merely frustration, or was it a touch of jealousy giving force to his cousin's words? "Did Miss Mary not thank you for your removal of Wickham from the garden?"

Richard reluctantly admitted that she had. "But," he protested, "her commendation of Mr. Collins had him broaching the idea of securing dances with her at the ball."

Perhaps it was just annoyance about the success of his planning being put in danger which had him grumbling about Collins.

"And..." Darcy prompted. He was positive that Richard was not the sort to let Mr. Collins be the first to gain assurance of a dance if he were bent on keeping the man from doing so.

"I can only dance with her twice. There are still plenty of other dances to be filled."

Darcy chuckled. It sounded like his cousin was more than a little put out with the idea of Miss Mary dancing any set with Mr. Collins. "Which two did you claim?"

"The first and the supper sets." He glanced over his shoulder at Darcy as he opened the door to his room, which was across the hall from Darcy's. "I thought those were the most important ones to secure."

"That seems reasonable. Those are the ones Elizabeth has promised me." Darcy held his door open and waited to see if Richard had more to say.

"Darcy!" Hurst came bounding up the stairs. "Colonel Fitzwilliam!"

Darcy had never seen Hurst move so quickly in the whole of their acquaintance.

"What has happened?"

"A carriage…" Hurst pointed towards the stairs as he took a gulping breath. "I heard what I thought was a carriage arriving while I was lying on the chaise and Louisa was muttering, in a rather unpleasant way, about Miss Elizabeth to Caroline." He shook his head as if he did not understand his wife. "She was a sweet girl before I married her."

Darcy had never found Louisa to be particularly sweet, but he was not about to say such to her husband.

"That is neither here nor there." He waved his previous comment away with his hand. "Louisa was just launching into the idea that Caroline turn her eyes in a different direction," he pointed at Richard, "when I peeked out the window and saw that what I had heard was indeed a carriage. And in this weather!"

"Who is it?" Richard asked. "Did you see who has come to call?"

"My son! I must see my son!" The words of their unexpected caller floated up the stairs and answered Richard's question.

"I believe, Cousin, that you are the only gentleman in residence with a mother," Darcy said.

Richard blew out a breath. "I suppose this means we will not be going to Longbourn."

"It also means you were wrong about the roads not being passible for a carriage," Hurst muttered. "If you had not claimed them to be in such dire condition, I am certain I could have convinced Louisa to take Caroline to Meryton to spend my money."

The three men walked toward the stairs.

"And my nephew. I must see my nephew as well. In a private room. We have family matters to discuss."

Darcy groaned. His aunt was using that tone she favoured when she was displeased.

"Mother, why are you here?" Richard asked from the top of the stairs before descending them faster than he had ascended them.

"And why are you running? We do not run in the house, Richard Fitzwilliam. I do not know how many times I have told you that, but I do know it has been from the moment you could walk and leave the nursery."

"Bingley does not care if I run down the stairs to find out why my mother has risked life and limb to drive a half day in treacherous weather."

"It is rain, not snow or ice. I hardly think it qualifies as treacherous weather." Her head tipped from side to side as if considering something. "I do suppose it was a trifle risky, for we did not drive nearly so fast as I wished for us to do."

"I am glad your coachman has some sense," Richard muttered.

"Give me a kiss, dear, and then, we will retire to a room to discuss matters at hand."

"Why are you here?"

"That is the matter at hand," she replied with a pointed look before tapping her cheek, which Richard kissed.

"Are you not going to remove your coat?"

"No." She looked past Richard to Darcy. "I do hope your welcome is better than the one I have received from my son."

"It is good to see you, my lady." Darcy gave her the required kiss that was indicated by another tap on her cheek.

She turned and held her hand out to Mr. Hurst, who took it and bowed.

"Would you be so kind, sir, as to tell Mr. Bingley and his sisters that I will require a room a day earlier than expected?"

"It would be my pleasure, my lady," Mr. Hurst replied before turning to leave them.

"I will not be using the room immediately as I do have some other business which needs my attention, but if the room could be made ready within the next hour," she called after him.

"What other business do you have?" Richard asked.

"That is also the matter at hand." She looked at Netherfield's butler. "A room, if you will."

The man bowed his head and said, "Follow me, my lady."

No sooner had Darcy, Richard, and Lady Matlock been ensconced in a small drawing room near the library than she turned to them with a smile. Her former displeasure seemed to have evaporated completely in the time it took to walk the short distance from the entry hall to this room.

"I hear my dearest wishes are to come true," she said.

Darcy looked at Richard and then his aunt. "Which wishes are those?"

"Why, that both you and my son have found brides, of course."

"I have not found a bride," Richard retorted.

"I hear it is only a matter of time until the young lady you seem fascinated by becomes your bride. That is why I am here and Lady Catherine is with your father. He is much better at dealing with his sister when she is put out than I am, and," she laughed lightly, "she is most certainly put out!" Again, she laughed lightly.

"Now, I am given to understand from her ladyship that Darcy was found embracing a lady in a garden and directly thereafter made her an offer of marriage." She pressed her lips together.

Darcy closed his eyes and shook his head. "I was not compromised, nor did I compromise any lady."

"That is not how your aunt tells it." Lady Matlock laughed fully at that. "Of course, I have never believed more than half of what Catherine says, so I did not believe you had been trapped by a fortune hunter – or worse become a reprobate."

"Is that how Aunt Catherine is telling it?"

Lady Matlock shook her head. "Oh heavens, no! I have taken a great deal of the dramatics from the presentation, I assure you." She turned to her son. "I understand both Darcy's lady and her sister, a Miss..." she tapped her lip as if she could not remember the name, though she was fooling no one, "Mary, I believe it was, is a gentleman's daughter but of little standing and poor presentation with only mediocre accomplishments."

Richard arched his left eyebrow and stared resolutely at his mother, who only smiled.

"Yes, I did not expect you to give me the information I wished. That is why I am still wearing my coat, and I suggest you get yours." She turned toward the door. "I plan to meet both ladies and form my own opinion." She paused a moment at the door. "Darcy, will you tell my driver where your lady resides, or should I gather that information from Bingley's butler?"

An hour later, Darcy found himself where he wanted to be – at Longbourn with Elizabeth at his side. Mrs. Bennet was, of course, beyond honoured to have Lady Matlock in her sitting room. He was certain that no one in the whole house was unaware of that fact since it had been declared more than once and at a volume that seemed proportionate to the lady's excitement.

His aunt had been hard pressed to contain her astonishment at Mrs. Bennet's exuberance. However, at present, Mrs. Bennet's voice was well-modulated to a private discussion, and the two ladies seemed to have found a common ground on which to converse as if they had been friends for years.

"Have you chosen a date for your nuptials?" Lady Matlock asked Darcy.

That was the common ground – weddings and matches. Both his aunt and his future mother-in-law had discovered a shared affinity for the married states of all those within their realm of influence.

"We have not, but I did have a date in mind. However, I have not had a chance to discuss it with my betrothed."

His aunt smiled. "She is here and so are you. I see nothing standing in the way of your settling this matter now. It will be so much easier then for us," here she looked at Mrs. Bennet, "to prepare what needs to be prepared to celebrate as we should."

"You expect me to discuss a date now?" In the sitting room, with everyone, including Mr. Collins, present? His aunt might wish it, but it was never going to happen!

"I do." She held his gaze for a moment before shifting to Elizabeth. "Do you have a preference for when you would like to marry?"

Elizabeth looked at Jane. "My sister and I had discussed, perhaps, sharing the day, but neither of us have spoken to our gentlemen about that."

"I have no issue with it being a joint affair." Bingley had not been willing to be left home with his sisters when there was a carriage braving the roads to Longbourn, and so he was also in the sitting room with Darcy. "What was the date you had in mind, Darcy? And please, do not say next year."

Mr. Bennet chuckled. "I agree with Mr. Bingley. Please do not make me endure discussions of wedding preparation for a year."

All eyes, including the finest pair he had ever seen, were turned towards Darcy, who shook his head.

"I refuse to state any date that I have not first discussed with Elizabeth."

"May we use your study, Papa?" Elizabeth asked.

"Most certainly, but do not be too long, or everything will be decided for you."

Darcy rose, followed Elizabeth to her father's study, and closed the door behind them, once they had entered.

"Do you have a preference for when we marry?" Darcy began.

Elizabeth shook her head. "I suppose I would like it if it were not at Christmas time. There is already so much that happens then, and I would not want our marriage to begin in a hurried fashion. I still have not met your sister, and you have not met my aunt and uncle Gardiner. They are joining us, as they do each year, for Christmas."

"And I will have Georgiana join me. I am relieved to hear your thoughts on the matter, for I was not wishing for a December wedding or even one at Twelfth Night as I know some like to do." He took her hands in his. "I was, in fact, hoping that we could marry on February sixteen, my birthday."

Her eyes grew wide. "Your birthday?" she repeated.

"Yes, my birthday." He smiled at her and said no more.

Her surprise-filled eyes quickly shifted to amusement. He loved the way her eyes sparkled as they were now.

"Do you have a reason for this wish?"

He lifted her hands to his lips. "It is not truly my wish so much as my father's."

Understanding dawned in her eyes. "The last letter's proposed deadline," she said with a nod of her head.

"Yes, that is why I chose the date. Well, that and the fact that your becoming my wife is the best gift I could ever receive." There would never be another birthday present he would treasure as greatly as the lady who stood before him – not even if he were to some day be blessed with a son or daughter on his birthday, for, even then, she would be the source of that joy.

"Then," an eyebrow arched over her dancing eyes while impertinence touched her smile, "I think that is the best day, and on this, I shall not be moved. Not for any inducement."

"Not if my aunt protests?" Which Darcy knew she might.

Elizabeth shook her head, and Darcy drew her into his embrace.

"Not even if my cousin breaks your sister's heart?" Again, it was not something outside the realm of possibilities.

"Not even then. I am afraid, Mr. Darcy, that there is nothing in this world that could keep me from my promise to you. You, my love, are stuck with me, unless, of course, you break our betrothal."

"I would never do that!"

She smiled as if she knew that to be true. "In that case, on February sixteenth, I will happily become your Mrs. Darcy. I only wish your father were here so I could thank him."

"On that we are most firmly agreed. Now, shall we go tell my aunt and your mother that they have nearly three months to prepare and your father that he has only that long to endure the preparations?" His gaze shifted from her eyes to her lips. Truth be told, he would rather not rush back to the sitting room. Whatever his aunt planned in his absence could be undone after a bit of arguing.

Elizabeth shook her head and smiled as if she could read his mind. "Not until after you have kissed me."

"Again," Darcy said with a chuckle, "I find we are of one mind." And with that, he pressed his lips to hers, enjoying, for a brief moment, a taste of the delight that would forever be his. For what would be his would be a lifetime of love and companionship, as well as of joy and sorrow and struggle and peace. All of which would be made more bearable and meaningful for having found her, his father's last and most precious gift.

Are you curious to fnd out what happens between Richard and Mary? Their story can be found in Sweet Extras, book 4, *Pretending to Love Mary*.

If you enjoyed this book, be sure to let others know by leaving a review.

~*~*~

Want to know when other Leenie books will be available?

You can always know what's new with my books by subscribing to my mailing list.

leeniebrown.com/subscribe

~*~*~

Turn the page to read an excerpt of another one of Leenie's books.

Her Father's Choice Excerpt

Prologue

OCTOBER 1811

Not handsome enough but with fine eyes? Mr. Bennet chuckled to himself as he tucked himself away in the corner of the drawing room at Lucas Lodge. From here he could keep an eye on his daughters and listen to various conversations as people moved from place to place. Most of them would, at one point or another, pass through the door near him to the room beyond where there was a table laid out with various forms of refreshment.

He chuckled again as he repeated Mr. Darcy's comment to Miss Bingley to himself. Fine eyes, indeed! His Lizzy possessed the most expressive eyes of any lady Mr. Bennet had ever met. One look let you know quite clearly what she was thinking.

"Fine eyes," he muttered. It was as he had suspected when he had first met Mr. Darcy — Elizabeth would make him a fine wife. It had not taken long for that reserved and well-educated gentleman to fall under the spell of a lady whose mind was just as astute as his own. Not handsome enough? The man must have been in some foul mood to have spoken so harshly and, he added with some force to himself, wrongly. Elizabeth was not Jane, but she was by no means lacking in beauty.

But that was the fly in the ointment. Elizabeth had heard the slight Mr. Darcy had made at the assembly and taken such a strong disliking to the man. Mr. Bennet sighed and shook his head. He knew that bringing the two together would be quite the undertaking — excessively difficult but utterly necessary if he wished to see Elizabeth well-matched and happy. Mr. Darcy was, in every way that Mr. Bennet could determine, the gentleman who was his daughter's equal.

"I tried to arrange a dance between them," said Sir William as he handed his long-time friend a glass of lemonade. "But, she is quite set against him, it seems."

"I saw," Mr. Bennet replied. "And then I heard him mention her fine eyes."

"Indeed?"

Bennet nodded. "Miss Bingley is quite put out by the comment. I do not envy his position of having an unhappy woman yapping at his elbow." He raised his eyebrows and smirked as he took a sip of his drink.

Sir William lifted his glass in salute. "Hear, hear. I have had it happen a time or two in the past eight and twenty years myself. There is nothing quite like the continual complaining of a disgruntled woman robed in supposed humour to try one's nerves."

"He is a patient one. I am sure I could not abide Miss Bingley's comments so graciously as he." Mr. Bennet shifted in his chair. "It is a good sign, for if he can tolerate Miss Bingley in a fit of pique, he should be able to handle my Lizzy."

"Aye, he should, but Lizzy's tongue and mind are a bit sharper. And her opinions are not so easily swayed." There was a hint of caution in Sir William's voice.

Mr. Bennet knew that his friend agreed with him about Mr. Darcy and Elizabeth making a fine match. That had not, however, stopped Sir William from voicing his concern, repeatedly, that Elizabeth could not be swayed from her current dislike of the gentleman.

"She will come around, although," Mr. Bennet drew out the word and lowered his voice, "that may not happen until after they are married."

Sir William laughed. "Exactly how do you propose we get her to marry him when she does not like him? Surely, you would not suggest a compromise?"

Mr. Bennet tapped his finger against the side of his glass. "I would do almost anything to assure the happiness of my

Lizzy, even if it meant bearing her anger and forcing her hand."

He watched Elizabeth, who was talking intently to her dear friend, Charlotte Lucas. He smiled as she sneaked a third glance at Mr. Darcy. If Mr. Bennet was not mistaken, and he rarely was when it came to understanding Elizabeth, she was fascinated by the man from Derbyshire. It was a fascination that he was certain was foreign to her.

"I pray it does not come to it, but if a compromise is necessary, can I count on your assistance?"

Sir William studied his friend and then Elizabeth for a moment. "You are convinced she will be happy?"

"Completely."

Sir William sighed. It was a sound of resignation and the same one he always made when he was about to bow to Mr. Bennet's wishes.

"Then, my friend," he said, "I will happily assist you with whatever you need."

Acknowledgements

THERE ARE MANY WHO have had a part in the creation of this story. Some have read and commented on it. Some have proofread for grammatical errors and plot holes. Others have not even read the story and a few, I know, will never read it.

First and foremost, I want to thank God for giving me the passion, ability, and opportunity to write.

Next, I want to say *thank you* to Zoe, Rose, Kristine, Ben, and Kyle. Your encouragement and belief in my ability, or simply your patience when I became cranky or when supper was late or the groceries ran low, was invaluable. I feel blessed through your help, support, and understanding.

Then, I would also like to say *thank you* to my Patreon patrons, who followed this story as it developed and waited, as patiently as one might do, from one Friday to the next, to read a new chapter. Every comment and typo catch has been so helpful. These few words cannot contain the amount of gratitude I feel for you constant support of my work. I'm excessively glad that I get to write with you by my side.

And finally, I want to thank my husband for, without his somewhat pushy insistence that I start sharing my writing, none of my writing goals and dreams would have been met. I love you dearly.

About Leenie

Leenie has always been a girl with an active imagination, which, while growing up, was both an asset, providing many hours of fun as she played out stories, and a liability, when her older sister and aunt would tell her frightening tales. At one time, they had her convinced Dracula lived in the trunk at the end of the bed she slept in when visiting her grandparents!

Although it has been years since she cowered in her bed in her grandparents' basement, she still has an imagination which occasionally runs away with her, and she feeds it now as she did then — by reading!

Her heroes, when growing up, were authors, and the worlds they painted with words were (and still are) her favourite playgrounds! Now, as an adult, she spends much of her time in the Regency world, playing with the characters from her favourite Jane Austen novels and those of her own creation.

When she is not traipsing down a trail in an attempt to keep up with her imagination, Leenie resides in the beautiful province of Nova Scotia with her two sons and her very own Mr. Brown (a wonderful mix of all the best of Darcy, Bingley, and Edmund with a healthy dose of the teasing Mr. Tilney and just a dash of the scolding Mr. Knightley).

More Books by Leenie

You can find all of Leenie's books at this link

bit.ly/LeenieBBooks
where you can explore the collections below

~*~

Dash of Darcy and Companions Collection

Marrying Elizabeth Series

Sweet Possibilities and Sweet Extras

Willow Hall Romances

The Choices Series

Darcy Family Holidays

Darcy and... An Austen-Inspired Collection

Teatime Tales (Sweet Austen-inspired Novelettes)

Other Pens

Touches of Austen

Nature's Fury and Delights (Sweet Regency Novelettes)

Connect with Leenie

Subscribe to Leenie's Mailing List:

leeniebrown.com/subscribe

Website:

leeniebrown.com

Patreon:

patreon.com/LeenieBrown

Facebook:

facebook.com/LeenieBrownAuthor

MeWe:

mewe.com/p/leeniebrown1

Instagram:

@leeniebbooks

E-mail: *LeenieBrownAuthor@gmail.com*